HOW
I GOT
SKINNY,
FAMOUS,
AND FELL MADLY
IN LOVE

Also by Ken Baker

Fangirl

HOW I GOT SKINNY, FAMOUS, AND FELL MADLY IN LOVE

KEN BAKER

RP | TEENS
PHILADELPHIA • LONDON

Books published by Running Press are available at special discounts for bulk
purchases in the United States by corporations, institutions, and other
organizations. For more information, please contact the Special Markets
Department at the Perseus Books Group, 2300 Chestnut Street, Suite 200,
Philadelphia, PA 19103, or call (800) 810-4145, ext. 5000, or e-mail
special.markets@perseusbooks.com.

ISBN 978-0-7624-5014-5
Library of Congress Control Number: 2013950638
E-book ISBN 978-0-7624-5203-3

9   8   7   6   5   4   3   2   1
Digit on the right indicates the number of this printing

Cover and interior design by T.L. Bonaddio
Edited by Lisa Cheng
Typography: ITC Cushing, Permanent Marker, Snickles, Futura, Univers,
LeagueGothic, Helvetica Neue, ITC Berkeley, Digital Dream, Abril Fatface

Published by Running Press Teens
An Imprint of Running Press Book Publishers
A Member of the Perseus Books Group
2300 Chestnut Street
Philadelphia, PA 19103–4371

Visit us on the web!
www.runningpress.com/kids

For anyone who has ever felt not good enough

FREE·DOM

NOUN

The power or right to act, speak, or think as one wants without hindrance or restraint.

MENU

I. APPETIZER

SUNDAY, OCTOBER 27

Another day, another driving "lesson" through the mean streets of Highland Beach. And it's a group effort with Mom shotgun and Angel riding appropriately in the Backseat Bitch Seat.

As I turn right onto Sea Spray Avenue, Mom scans the row of McMansions for sale. "Look at all the signs! All foreclosures. It's like no one can afford to live in California anymore. Honestly, Highland is going to hell in a sand basket."

"*Hand* basket," I correct her.

"Oh, right," she says. "Well, whatever. You know what I'm saying."

"It's just depressing," she continues. "Your dad has lost almost half his clients in the last year. When money gets tight, people stop taking care of their bodies. Another six months and everyone in this town is gonna be a big fat pig!"

Mom puts her hand in front of her mouth, as if trying to catch the F-bomb she just dropped onto the lap of myself, her fat daughter. But I don't flinch. Instead, I just keep driving, my elbows resting atop the rolls of blubber that billow out from the sides below my bra like squishy armrests.

She taps the tip of her right heel on the floor mat. I would tell her she probably has Restless Leg Syndrome, but then she would just use it as an excuse for another prescription and two more days a week with her shrink.

Despite her flaws, I do love her. How could I not? She wants nothing more than for her two daughters to be happy (aka "skinny" like her) and to follow in their mother's footsteps and not have to get a real job like in an office, or something horribly civilian like that.

Even though Mom's got a heart of gold—okay, more like a heart of *platinum*—when you look up "Hot Mess" in the dictionary, it should read "Brandi Jackson" accompanied by a picture of Mom being wheeled out of her facelift surgery last summer with white gauze bandages wrapped around her face like some sort of MILF mummy.

Sea Spray comes to an end at Coastal Highway. I roll gradually to a stop, look both ways, and execute a perfectly vectored left turn. Locals call this stretch of CH the "coronary row." Pretty much every greasy, artery-clogging eatery is located here, making this what I call My Favorite Place in the World.

There's In-N-Out, where normally I like to order two "Double-Doubles," large fries, and a chocolate shake. And there's Old Faithful: Mickey D's and its to-die-for vanilla shakes and Big Macs with blissful special sauce. Across the street sits the twofer culinary heaven of Carl's Jr. and the Green Burrito, a genius concept featuring an all-American burger joint and a Mexican eatery—under the very same roof! Then there's Carl's

Jr., whose Double Western Bacon Cheeseburger and its glorious stack of two beef patties, two slices of American cheese, crispy onion rings, and "tasty BBQ sauce on a toasted sesame seed bun" is so good California should legally classify it as a narcotic.

Technically, I'm not allowed to go to such dens of deliciousness anymore, at least not since Dr. Hung read me the riot act a couple months ago. That's when our family doctor informed me my daily lunch delight of the Double Western Bacon Cheeseburger and its one-thousand calories (half of which come from saturated—aka "bad"—fat) were in large part responsible for making me more than fifty pounds overweight and, "clinically speaking," an obese tub of lard.

That's right, kids. I'm officially the Big O. And I don't mean Oprah.[1]

After my exam, Dr. Hung even opened up his iPad to show me something called a "BMI Chart." It apparently explained that I was five foot six inches, 192.2 pounds, with a "BMI" (Body Mass Index) of 31, which meant I was basically yet another large-and-in-charge teenage American statistic.

The doctor probably didn't want to hurt my feelings. Never once did he drop the F-bomb. Instead, he tried to make me feel better by using synonyms like "an unhealthy weight" and handed me a pamphlet that said 17 percent of all teens are obese. Apparently, texting and video gaming doesn't burn calories like it used to.

Let's face it, "obese" is a very polite term, but the bottom line is that it was Dr. Hung's way of informing me that I am so big I could have my own zip code . . . so big that skydivers could

---

[1] Allegedly obese.

use my panties for parachutes . . . so big that my butt could get me arrested at an airport for carrying 200 pounds of crack.

Thick. Heavy. Big-boned. Plump. Full-figured. Chunky. Womanly. Large. Curvy. Plus-size. Husky. I've been pretty much called it all at one point or another. By the time you get to high school, most people have learned it's not nice to hurt people's feelings and so they come up with words that won't break your chubby little heart.

Plus, by the time you turn sixteen and you've spent your whole life in a pretty-people city like Highland Beach, where the official municipal logo depicts a surfer and bikini-clad volleyball player prancing beneath a yellow sunburst, you've learned that being overweight is tantamount to being Bin Laden—you know, sexually speaking. Add the fact that my father is a former L.A. Laker and now full-time workout freak who hasn't eaten a potato chip in seventeen years, let alone a juicy burger with onion rings, and you can imagine that I would have to be wickedly in denial not to realize I am a skinny-challenged individual.

I know I'm fat, okay? Unlike Angel, my fashion choices are limited to whatever I can find online or at Sears and JCPenney (aka Not-Cute Clothing Stores). I know the mean girls at Highland High think it's funny to giggle behind my back about how my gut hangs over the elastic waistband of my pants, an unsightly phenomenon that in seventh grade earned me the unfortunate nickname "Muffin Top." I also know that guys—except for my amazing boyfriend, Ben—treat me like I am sexually invisible. I may be a lot of things, but I am definitely not in denial about my public image.

Cruising right through CH's fast-food nirvana with my mom isn't helping to curb my appetite for globular goodness. I try not to look at those golden arches, and luckily the waft of vegetable oil gurgling from the fryers doesn't make its way inside our car. This has become my life: a series of small victories based on trying my best not to eat food I know is bad for me but that I enjoy as much as my sister enjoys wearing skimpy bikinis with dental-floss butt patches.

"I think the costume store is up here on the right," Mom says. "Slow down. Remember, gradually like."

I tap up the turn-signal handle and hook a sharp right into the parking lot of the strip mall. We're shopping for my Halloween costume. My family is a bunch of Halloween freaks, so much so that every year my parents host a party at our house. And yet, I still don't have a costume.

My older sister, Angel, who picked out her costume weeks ago, stays in the car, texting her new boyfriend. Mom and I step inside, where the store looks more like a sex shop than a costume store. Sexy nurses. Sexy cats. Sexy cops. Sexy cowgirls and Indians. Stripper shoes and stripper shorts. But in the back of the store, wedged next to the kids' costumes, are a few racks of decidedly unsexy outfits for adults—and big girls like me.

"There's Chewbacca!" Mom grabs the furry creature from the rack and hands it to me. I look at the tag. It's a size medium. I shake my head and hand it back to her. "Too small, huh?" she says in a conspicuously nonjudgmental tone. "Well, let's keep looking."

Mom rifles through and finds an XL and holds it up to me.

"This should work," she says. It doesn't. Turns out it's a youth XL. Too small.

The pickings are quite slim in the *Star Wars* section. I see a couple of Stormtroopers and an Obi-Wan Kenobi, and also some larger-size Princess Leias and Darth Vaders made of material that looks about as comfortable as construction paper.

"Do you have any Han Solos?" I ask the clerk, who is dressed as Pocahontas.

"Um, I think we got some fake hands in aisle six," she says, smacking a wad of overly pungent peppermint gum.

"*Han* Solos," I repeat slowly. "Like the guy in *Star Wars*. You know, Chewbacca's sidekick." She has a Confused Puppy Face. "My boyfriend wants to be Han Solo." The chick stares at me like I'm speaking a language she doesn't understand—such as, say, English.

"I don't know. Whatever we have is on the racks. There's no, like, secret stash or anything."

It really is hard to find good help these days.

"You need to find Ben something appropriate for the couples theme," Mom says as the useless store chick walks back to the register.

Last year's theme was "historical." That meant we had a lot of bearded Abe Lincolns and white-wig George Washingtons stumbling around. I came as Our Lord and Savior Jesus Christ. You might think that "Halloween" is enough of a theme for a costume party, but no, no, no. Not at the Jackson household, where making things more complicated than they need to be is taken very seriously.

I go to plan B and wander the store as my mom tries on a

pair of Lucite stripper heels. A few minutes later, I find costume gold buried in a bin underneath a pile of cheap masks.

I walk over to Mom and slide a white plastic mask onto my head.

"What's that?" she asks, confused.

"Quack, quack." I fashion my elbows into wings.

"A duck?" she guesses.

"No." I slide the mask up and rest it on my head. "I'm a duck face."

"What's a duck face?" she asks.

"You know, that model face Angel makes when she's posing for a picture." I pucker my lips and push them outward like a come-hither Daffy Duck. "Sexy, huh?"

Mom rolls her eyes and sighs. "Whatever makes you happy, Emery. And if putting other people down to make yourself feel better does it for you, that's your choice."

Ignore.

I text Ben. He's working at his parents' surf shop down by the pier.

> Ur gonna love my costume. But for u: No Han Solo, sorry 😞 —Just Darth or Princess Leia. Pick 1

It only takes him about 4.8 seconds to reply. Must be a slow day down at the pier.

> Def go w Leia

Gosh, I really do love Ben. And not only because he's up for wearing a curly-Q hairdo wig, not just because he is the only boy who has ever found me attractive, but mostly because his XXL-size costume, which will barely fit his giant body, comparatively, makes me feel like a totally skinny babe.

MONDAY, OCTOBER 28

My mom watches a lot of TV. And I really do mean "TV." As in the 57-inch mega-appliance with the flat-glass screen screwed to the wall of our living room like some sort of monument to Best Buy. Unlike most modern-day human beings, Mom never watches videos on a computer or—gasp!—a phone.

Another way that Mom kicks it old school is that she actually pays attention to commercials—and totally believes the propaganda in them. In fact, the commercials make more of an impression on her than do the shows. It doesn't matter what's being sold. If the commercial makes it look super awesome, she will plunk down a credit card on the spot or write it down on a piece of paper, and the next time she is shopping, she'll buy it.

Fabric softener that makes your sheets as soft as a baby's bottom! Skin moisturizer that erases years from your face! Breakfast cereal that will get your family making a fast break to start their day! There really is no product in the consumer universe my mother couldn't be convinced she just absolutely needs to have. A few years ago, when our garage filled up floor-to-ceiling with boxes of crap she had ordered from watching Home Shopping Network, my dad, in a rare show of balls, had HSN blocked from our cable.

Mom's gullibility explains why, after suffering through an already very long day, we are now standing in an absurdly long line on a sidewalk. We are numbers sixteen and seventeen waiting for our lucky chance to step up to the glass-encased counter and order deli sandwiches that leave you feeling about as satisfied as a Twitter addict whose keyboard is missing the "@" key.

"What kind of bread, dear?" Mom asks, patting my back like I'm three.

"Does it really matter? They all taste like cardboard."

"Emery." Mom hikes her black Gucci purse back up her right shoulder and crosses her arms. "Don't be so negative."

The green-and-yellow glow of this glorified cafeteria contains all the charm of a highway rest stop. To be fair, the so-called "Subway diet" is popular; my mom isn't the only fool convinced that these sandwiches are healthier than they really are. The people in front of us look excited as they tell the poor dude behind the counter exactly what they want.

I've left my phone in the car (by accident, trust me) and so have nothing to distract me from the pain. No texting with Ben. No checking Instagram to see what fascinating pictures my friends might have posted in the last eight minutes since I last saw them at school.

I look past Mom and across the parking lot to Carl's Jr., which I can see through the glass. Carl's is totally empty, mouth-wateringly ready for me to come and order my favorite burger with large fries and a Coke. Mom notices me staring in the direction of the Temple of Tastiness. When I glance back at her, her eyes dart forward nervously.

"Don't worry, Mom." I pat her on the back. "I'm not eating there."

"Well, good," she chirps. We have since moved closer to the front—close enough to get a glimpse at the "fresh" bread choices.

"Wheat," Mom thinks aloud, though there are still five people, including a bratty seven-year-old girl, ahead of us. "With turkey maybe." She purses her lips. "Then again, I probably shouldn't have bread."

A few minutes that seem like hours later, it is our turn. The little brat in front of us has just ordered the most complex sandwich ever made—with pickles and olives and lettuce (toasted) with provolone cheese and pepperoni (but NOT salami) and just a little bit of vinegar and a squirt of mustard. Intricate stuff for a second grader.

Finally, Mom steps to the counter and places her well-rehearsed order.

"I'll have a turkey sub," Mom says. "Without bread."

"Excuse me?" replies the poor man behind the counter. "I don't understand."

"A turkey sub with . . . no . . . bread," she repeats slowly.

"*Okaaaay . . .*" The confused soul in clear plastic gloves struggles. "So you want a salad."

"No, no, no. I'm sorry, but I don't like your salads." Mom smiles. "I would simply like turkey, avocado, lettuce—lots of lettuce—and tomato."

The poor guy shrugs his shoulders and shakes his head, then grabs a bowl and starts filling it with her order. Mom peers through the glass.

"I had two pieces of toast for breakfast." She rubs her stomach. "Too many carbs. I'm done with bread for the day. Protein time."

Mom shuffles along the food line, down closer to the register, and I step forward, peering through the glass at the offerings.

"Good afternoon," I say.

"What kind of bread?" the traumatized worker asks wearily.

"You pick," I say. "Whatever you want, sir."

The man turns to reach for the rack behind him. Midreach he suddenly stops, turns to me, and says, "Excuse me?"

"Pick my bread." I point to the silver trays stacked against the back wall. "I trust you."

He shoots an anxious glare at Mom, who is standing, eyes bulging. Mom doesn't like to leave anything to chance. She is a perfectionist. A complete-and-utter control freak. She's the lady who made a checklist from the first day of kindergarten that she taped on my mirror reading:

DAILY TO DO!!!

☐ Make bed

☐ Get dressed

☐ Brush teeth

☐ Use bathroom

☐ Eat breakfast (glass of soy milk)

☐ Lunch, hand sanitizer, snack, and homework in backpack

By the time I was in seventh grade, Mom stopped making lists because I stopped paying attention to them. Angel, on the other hand, still loves lists. But her morning to-do has been replaced with more big-picture goals, such as the one she keeps taped to the wall next to her bathroom mirror. . . .

MY LIFE TO DO!!!

- ☐ Be famous
- ☐ Always have perky boobs and a small butt
- ☐ Maintain weight "under 120 lbs" AT ALL TIMES
- ☐ Host own TV show by age 22
- ☐ Make cover of *Sports Illustrated* Swimsuit Issue by age 21
- ☐ Marry pro athlete by age 27
- ☐ Have two babies (Jasper Jr. and Amber)

"Lists help organize your thinking and focus you to achieve your dreams," Mom has always said. I've always been confused by this idea of following your so-called dreams. I mean, the only dreams I remember are nightmares that may or may not involve sketchy, inappropriate sex scenarios involving teachers and random guys. Hardly the stuff of list-making inspiration.

Anyway, you can understand that my mom is left mortified when I dare leave such an important choice as what carbohydrate I would have wrapped around my processed meat to a total stranger in a hairnet and green smock. I know this because her face is so white that the blood has clearly dropped from her face to her tanned, wickedly moisturized knees.

The poor guy locks eyes frightfully with Mom.

"Seriously, sir, just pick whatever you think tastes best," I insist.

"Wheat," he says/asks.

I shrug.

"So, um," he says. "*Wheeeeat* you want?"

"Sure!" I reply. "Wheat sounds healthy and fresh to me!"

Mom bites her bottom lip and looks away.

The worker finishes my sandwich and then asks the question that certainly must ruin Mom's day: "Mayonnaise or mustard?"

"Mayo." Before Mom can critique my condiment, I add, "And, oh, some cheese."

"What kind?" the man asks.

"America's finest will do, thanks."

As he layers on slices of unnaturally yellow cheese, I grab a bag of chips on the shelf next to the register and place them on the counter.

Mom huffs and looks away.

"What?" I ask her.

"We talked about this, Emery." Her delightful tone belies her frustration. She clenches her obnoxiously white teeth.

A long, awkward, icy Mother-Daughter pause.

"Remember? Emery. You know . . ."

"They're *baked* Lay's," I argue. "They're not gonna kill me."

"What about the cheese? The mayonnaise?" She counts the sins with her fingers. "The bread. You just managed to make a healthy sandwich unhealthy. I give up."

WEDNESDAY, OCTOBER 30

"Team meeting!" Mom yells up to us from the bottom of the stair-case. "Dad's ready. Come to the kitchen. Now, girls!"

"Coming, Mommy!" Angel cheers from her bedroom like the good kids do on the Disney Channel. I eye roll when I hear her precious little manicured feet tapping down the hardwood floor in the hallway.

Did you know there are *thirty-two* fries (approximately) in a small McDonald's order? I do. I know this because I ran out of the contraband reward I had been giving myself for every math problem I had solved correctly.

Having accomplished my fry feat, I moved on to reading *A Mystery of Heroism*. It's for my English class report due at the end of the week. I wish Algebra, Spanish, AP Biology, and U.S. History were as interesting as English class.

The story is about a soldier in the heat of a major battle who has the brilliant idea of running into the middle of an open field being bombarded by bombs in order to fill a bucket of water for him and his fellow soldiers. Water was to him probably like a juicy Double-Double with bacon is to me, so I can relate.

"Emery!" Mom yells. "C'mon! Daddy's waiting."

I put down the book and walk downstairs. Mom and Angel are already huddled around the laptop on the island counter talking to Dad on Skype.

"Angel got a callback on that website hosting job," Mom tells him. "It's down to her and two other girls."

"So proud," Dad says, his voice echoing in his hotel room in Whatever City, USA. "Fingers, toes, and eyes crossed." He focuses his eyes noseward and Angel giggles. Their mutual cutesy/corny sense of humor never ceases to annoy me, especially when it is over her getting a job that requires her to merely look pretty and read what someone else has written. Does that really qualify as talent? I have been reading to people since Dr. Seuss in kindergarten and I'm not asking anyone to pay me for it.

"What's the name of the website?" I ask Angel.

"HotBuzzz," she replies. "One word. Three z's."

"Wow," I nod. "That extra z makes it sound so cool and hip. And awesome."

"Well, Angel, you've worked so hard to get to this point," Dad says. "And you know what Bruce says about hard work . . ."

"Of course, Daddy. Bruce[2] says, 'The only way you are going to get anywhere in life is to work hard at it.'"

"Boom!" Mom high-fives Angel as I sit at the countertop and do my best not to regurgitate a fry.

"Emery's here." Mom adjusts the laptop camera so he can

---

[2] As in Bruce Jenner of *E!* fame. Dad's reverence for All Things Bruce is only dwarfed by my mom's obsession with Bruce's wife, Kris Jenner, reality momager extraordinaire.

see me, and I slow-motion princess-wave my right hand.

Dad soldier-salutes me. "Hey, Em. Glad you could join us."

"Okay, Team Jackson," Mom announces. "Since Dad's gotta get back to his speech, let's hustle through this. How is Omaha, by the way, Jasper?"

"Cold. Real cold." Dad is wearing a black wool sweater. He turns his laptop cam to the window of his hotel room. "See the snow? We had flurries this morning. But honestly, I've got an amazing group of motivated ladies here. In fact, I have my final speech in fifteen minutes downstairs in the ballroom."

"What's your speech about, dear?" Mom asks.

"Resisting temptation."

Yeah, I'm tempted to go refill on small fries and get back to algebra.

"That's great, Jasper," Mom replies. Mom adores Dad so much it is cute. But kind of sad at the same time. Maybe because Dad doesn't look at her the same way she does at him.

Sometimes I wish I could have been there when the two met. They seem so happy in the pictures. Back then, Mom would spend her days doing auditions as a wannabe actress, and at night she worked as a "Laker Girl," as in one of the cheerleaders who dances in skimpy outfits on the court during time-outs and at halftime, all for the viewing pleasure of dirty old men.

Dad, meanwhile, had a front-row seat to his future wife's cheerleading performances. He was, after all, a six-foot-one benchwarmer with little to do but stare at the court as the coach drew up plays for the real players. Dad prefers to call himself "a depth player," a reserve forward for a team that was filled with superstars.

Whenever I see pictures of my parents from that time, just a couple years before I was born, I study their faces, searching to find what qualities I have from both. From Mom the similarities are obvious: dark, deep-set eyes; dark hair; chipmunk cheeks; and a forehead the size of Texas. But I see none of Dad's angular face, none of his blond hair, or his tall, lanky body in me.

When we were little, Angel, who does have most of these genetic blessings, would taunt me, saying that my chubbiness was the result of a genetic mutation. It bothered me until I realized that I could read four grade levels above her and that I was so smart that she would trade me food for me doing her homework.

I can only assume Angel gets her intellectual shortcomings from Mom, who, to this day, remains a MILF—and I'd say this even if she didn't freeze her face with Botox every three months. Even so, I notice she puts on makeup before we dial up Dad and I kind of feel sad that even after almost twenty years of marriage, she still feels the need to wear, basically, a mask in front of him. I wonder if she does it because she knows her handsome, motivational-speaking husband is spending the weekend surrounded by happiness-seeking desperate housewives fawning over him.

"Okay," Mom continues. "Let's get going here, Team. Now, I talked to Doc earlier today and he suggested that we, as a family, conduct a Brand Audit. This will help us better define who we are, which in turn will help us create a show that is unique and *singular* to us." She's using air quotes again. Major pet peeve of mine. But until I graduate next year and move out of the house and on with my life, I must endure such motherly annoyances.

I notice in the video box that Dad's staring offscreen, zoning out. Having trouble paying attention to mom's monologues is at least one thing my dad and I have in common. "I want each of us to come up with one word that sums up our personal brand.

"So, Jasper," Mom instructs. "You go first."

"Well," Dad thinks aloud. "Brandi, there are a lot of words that come to mind. Such as perfection . . . excellence . . . inspiration . . . motivation. But is there one word that sums up Jasper Jackson? It has to be Work! Because if you wanna live your dreams, if you want to achieve any darn thing in life, then you first gotta do The Work."

"That's right, Daddy," Angel says. "There's no substitute for hard work."

I look over Mom's shoulder and she scribbles in her notepad, "Dad = Work." She puts her pen down and gazes upward at the fake crystal chandelier.

"All righty, I'll go next," Mom says. "I was thinking my brand should be—pay attention here, guys—Brandi. What do you think?"

"That's lame," I say under my breath reflexively.

"Excuse me?" Mom twitches. "What did you say?"

"Nothing," I lie.

"What do you mean 'nothing'?" Mom parks her hands on her hips. "I heard you say something. If you have anything to share, please share with the team."

"Yes, Emery," Dad chimes in. "There is no 'I' in our team. We are democratic."

"I thought we were Republicans?" Angel says.

"I said 'democratic,' Angel pie," Dad baby-talks. "Not Democrats."

Although I can tell she still doesn't know the difference,

Angel offers up an unconvincing "oh, okay" as I start trolling Pinterest on my phone, searching "crazy cat photos" to spare me the boredom of this Team Meeting for Dummies.

"As I was saying," Mom goes on. "My brand is me! I represent myself. Even though our next project is to come up with a slogan, I already have mine: You can't say 'Brandi' without saying 'Brand.'"

Extremely pleased with her narcissistic answer, she quickly writes it down and turns to the blonde wonder to my left. "This is fun, isn't it, Angel? Your turn."

"Beauty," Angel answers without hesitation. "My brand is Beauty."

"Inside and out," Dad cheerfully adds.

"That's right," Angel agrees. "I personify beauty."

If I told you that in our weekly team meetings my family has me go last because they like to save the best for last, I would be lying. They have me go last because they have learned the hard way that if I go first, I will totally kill their buzz.

Mom turns to me. She's clenching her teeth again. "And you, Em? What is the one—and only one—word that defines your brand?" She looks down at her paper. Angel is looking at her reflection in a spoon. I look at the computer screen and see Dad zoning out with glassy eyes.

There's a part of me that wants to give them the answer they want to hear. They want me to say something reality TV–friendly like "honesty" or "humor" or "unpredictable." They want me to be the kind of character that makes unscripted TV so watchable. But unfortunately for them, the part of me that wants to give them what they want to hear always loses as soon as I open my mouth.

"Fat," I say matter-of-factly. "My brand is Fat."

My answer lingers like one of our dearly departed, floppy-eared old beagle Sunny's stinky farts on a hot summer night.

More silence. I am the elephant in the room.

"That's your answer," Angel sneers. She blows a pocket of air from her mouth. "Wow. Your final answer is Fat?"

"I didn't realize this was *Jeopardy!*" I reply. "But that's right, Alex! My final answer is Fat." I get up from the stool. "You know, we can brand that. I could have a whole line of Fat products. Fat-tastic milkshakes. Fat-tacular cheesecake. Fat-a-licious cookies. Just think of the possibilities!"

Angel gets up and storms out of the kitchen. Mom doesn't even bother to write down my answer and quickly gives Dad an obligatory "I loveya" and hangs up.

As I stand there proud of myself, my thoughts turn to something even more satisfying. There are chocolate chip cookies that Mom has hidden in the back of the pantry, stuffed away for tomorrow's Halloween party. And I am going to eat them. All of them.

THURSDAY, OCTOBER 31

"Why does everyone have to dress like a hooker on Halloween?" Angel is eyeballing the costumed partiers packed into our living room. "So typical."

Angel says this, mind you, while she herself stands in black fishnets under a white minidress with a hemline that comes up to her hip flexors. She is five foot ten inches and weighs 119.3 pounds. (I know this only because she tells me every day what she weighs in each morning on a digital scale.)

Angel sneaks a look in the living-room mirror, pressing her chest together and squeezing it skyward with her hands like she was playing an accordion or something. "I don't get it, Emery. Why are some people so desperate?"

"You're not exactly dressed like a nun."

"What?" Her eyes are still locked on the mirror. "I'm a nurse. So?"

The only thing indicating that she is supposed to be a nurse is her white hat with the Red Cross on the front. Otherwise she looks more like something out of a teenage boy's perverted hospital fantasy that gives a whole new meaning to "health care provider."

I have a very well thought-out theory about sexually risqué Halloween Ho'ness, which basically boils down to this: Girls like to dress like hos because on Halloween you want to be something that you are not. It is just not socially acceptable to dress like a prostitute. It is something you can't be the other 364 days of the year, but it is totally fine on the night of October 31. And if a girl really is a ho, then on Halloween she dresses like *more* of a ho. I mean, everyone wants to be hot and sexy, and what's the most over-the-top way to do this? Dress like a ho.

Girls shouldn't be hated for Halloween Ho'ness. Instead, we should celebrate each other on this special night. Girls too often hate on other girls, and especially on Halloween. This should be the one night they don't. But, alas, they do, and Angel is one of the haters, even though she is just as guilty as the rest of them.

Angel perceives her life to be everything that it is not. For example, she thinks she is fat, even though she is skinny. She thinks people love her, even though they talk crap behind her back. She thinks that her friends hang out with her because she is such an awesome person, but in actuality they do it because she is hot and thus hot guys hang around her and thus they hang out with her to meet said hot guys.

Robbie is Angel's obnoxious man-candy date for the night. Robbie-meister is also "an aspiring model" according to his Facebook profile that I creeped on after meeting him. He puts his steroidal right arm around her and with his other hand presses his fake stethoscope on her cleavage.

"*Hellooooo*, nurse," he growls. "Wanna play doctor?" Angel pushes him away and grimaces as if she is disgusted. Even though she is not. Robbie is twenty; Angel is eighteen. Their median emotional maturity: age six.

Angel presses her ample boobs together (again) and adjusts them (again), grunting in frustration because they won't stay together like they do in the magazines. Angel has perfect breasts. Their shape, their size—everything is, well, off-the-rack perfect.

Her breasts are a big reason why she has been making $1,000 a day modeling swimsuits for the last two years. She has the best boobs my parents' money could buy. After complaining for two years about being flatter than Kansas, Angel's dream came true. They were her seventeenth birthday present last spring. Angel calls them "Thelma and Louise."[3]

Mrs. Page across the street, the one who goes to church every Sunday at St. Boniface, thinks my mom is committing child abuse by letting a teenager get a boob job before her body has even fully developed. She said as much in a letter she left at our door when she found out a few months ago. Mom responded with her own, much shorter letter, reading, "Dear Mrs. Page, Go fu*# yourself. Love, Mrs. Jackson."

I have felt Thelma and Louise. I had to know what foreign objects felt like when surgically implanted on top of a teenage girl's breastplate. And you know what they feel like? Exactly like you'd think two foreign objects resting on top of a teenage girl's

---

[3] A) Angel has nicknamed her boobies and B) Angel's the kind of person who thinks it's okay to call homeless people "bums."

breastplate would feel like: cantaloupes.

Robbie grabs Angel by the hand, and when they start making out, I turn my back and scan the party.

The annual soiree is hopping as usual. Mom and Dad—dressed like a referee and a football player, respectively—are working the room with all the glad-handing ease of the First Family at a White House state dinner. Their Halloween costume party has become *the* social event of the fall in the slums of Highland Beach, complete with a photographer snapping pictures of everyone for the *Highland Beach Reporter*.

"Here ya go." Ben hands me a glass of sparkling cider and adjusts his Leia wig. I lift up my duck-face mask and set it atop my head so I can drink. Ben's Leia earmuffs look like hairy puff pastries. "Here's to George Lucas!" he toasts. "And to duck faces!" We clink our glasses in a toast and sip the wonder that is the nonalcoholic beverage of choice for us underagers while the adults drink their beer, wine, and champagne.

Just then, Josh, a senior, and one of my sister's moronic, drunk football player pseudo-friends, bumps into Ben, causing Ben to spill his drink on his own shirt and drop his glass onto the floor, shattering it into dozens of jagged little pieces. "Oops," the dumb jock says. "Sorry, fatso."

Ben bends over picking up the broken glass shards and can't hear Josh over the noise of the party. But I can.

"Hey," Josh says, pushing Ben in the back. "I said, 'I'm sorry, FATSO!'"

I wish Ben would stand up and punch the plastic green wreath off the toga-wearing tool, then knee him in the groin and make him squeal like a pig in front of his lobotomized blonde girlfriend. But he doesn't. So I take over.

"Hey, Josh." The jocky cretin turns around and grazes my gut with his hand. He stares at me and says, "What?"

"Oh, I was just wondering something. Can I ask you a question?"

"Emery, go blow yourself." Josh has always been a charmer, even back in sixth grade when the cops busted him for drinking beer at the beach.

"I would if I could reach," I shoot back. Josh's face remains as blank as copy paper. Clearly, the joke has gone over his head. Numb nut.

I angrily squint my eyes. "Ever wonder what your life would be like if your mom didn't drink alcohol when she was pregnant with you?"

One of Josh's friends spits out his drink mid sip in laughter and says, "Now that's funny."

But Josh looks confused—more confused than his normal look of befuddlement. "What's so funny?" he asks his buddy, who just shrugs and fights a war with his facial muscles trying not to laugh again.

Josh leans in and whispers in my ear. "Be careful. I've got pictures."

My heart starts racing. I turn my back to Ben and Josh's ogre pals.

"Pictures of what?" I ask.

"Us," he says with a creepy smile.

No way. I don't remember a camera. Must be a lie. He's gotta be lying. Please, dear God, make him be lying! I'm sorry I dressed as Jesus Christ last year for Halloween. I beg you, please, God, NO PICTURES!

Suddenly, Ben steps between me and Josh. "Let's all just take a deep breath and relax here," Ben calmly offers. "We're all friends. Just take 'er easy."

"I was relaxing—until this *thing* bumped into me, bro."

"Hey, it was just an accident." Ben focuses his attention back to the glass shards on the floor and pushes them into a pile with his foot. "I will clean this up."

Ben's gentlemanly response is both endearing and pathetic at the same time. When you've spent your whole life being kicked around for being the fat kid, this is who you become: a pushover. It's probably either this or turn into a serial killer.

Ben gathers up the last shards of glass with a napkin. Meanwhile, Josh shakes his head and stomps off to the balcony.

I kneel beside Ben and help him gather the glass pieces. "What was Josh whispering to you?" Ben asks.

"Nothing."

"Didn't look like nothing," he presses.

"Well, okay, he was saying something. But since I don't speak Moron I couldn't understand him."

Ben smiles and walks to the kitchen with the glass piled on the napkin. That's when I notice that a "pirate" has been standing beside us the entire time watching. He steps up to me.

"I'm Doc." He's wearing a black bandanna on his head with an eye patch, and he's leaning on a cane. "I must ask you. And forgive me if this comes across as rude, but I just want to ask you a simple question. Are you happy, Emery?"

Doc. He is the salt-and-pepper-bearded British guy whom my mom supposedly met at the lobby bar of Shine Hotel in downtown Highland a few months ago. As she tells the story, Doc started bragging to her about how he produces so-called "unscripted" TV shows. By the end of their conversation the sweet-talking producer, whose real name is "Marvin Harris" according to his Wikipedia page, had convinced Mom that our four-person freak show of a family could be cable-TV gold.

"Well"—I sigh—"I mean, my name could be Marvin, so things could be worse."

He doesn't react.

"All right, *soooo*." I hate awkward silences. "Why are you even here? Besides the free drinks and fabulous company."

"I wanted to meet the Jackson family that your mom has told me so much about."

I am really not in in the mood for this small talk with Doc. But since Ben is still in the other room, and I'm curious to know more about this guy, I tolerate the conversation.

"So *Doc*," I begin. "Why 'Doc'?"

Marvin flashes a toothy grin that reveals the most revoltingly busted row of yellowed chompers. Nasty.

"It's short for 'Documentary,'" he says in an accent à la Prince William, minus the good looks and nice teeth. "It hearkens back to my documentary filmmaking days. I won many film festival prizes, and that bloody name just stuck."

"Now," he says, "may I ask *you* a question?"

"News flash: You just did!" I break into giggles before stopping my bratty self. "Just kidding. Go ahead and ask away."

"What does freedom mean to you?" Yes, he fashions air quotes with his fingers when he says "freedom." What a cheese ball.

"Sir Marvin, that's a totally deep question coming from a reality TV show producer."

"Please, Emery," he says calmly. "Don't take this the wrong way, darling. I'm just trying to get to know you better. Your lovely mother has told me so much about you."

Hopefully by "so much," he doesn't mean as in how I wet the bed till I was eight years old, that in the last three years I ballooned from a thirty-inch to a forty-four-inch waist, and that I awkwardly had sex for the first time with Ben in a tent while on a camping trip four months ago. I ask him for clarification just in case.

"A lot?"

"She has told me of your struggles, that's all."

I just smile and lie. "I'm totally okay, thanks."

He fixes his stare at me. "Really, my dear. Are you really okay? It would seem to me that you are something of a prisoner of your own physicality."

"Wow. Who died and made you Aristotle?"

"I just think that your parents and I just want you to enjoy freedom."

"Well, freedom would mean being able to wear whatever I want, go wherever I want, play whatever sport I want, and just be whoever I want."

I think of adding that freedom would also be not having to be the only girl in the room right now who can't dress like a ho on Halloween because she's too fat, but while I'm brash and candid enough to say such a thing, I don't have the energy to explain my "Unified Theory of Halloween Hos" to this Brit with bad beer breath.

"Look . . ." He takes a sip from his beer and smiles. "Emery, you're a pretty girl, a positively delightful personality . . ."

Here it comes.

"And you have such a . . ."

Backhanded compliment coming in three, two, one.

". . . big personality and a really pretty face.

"And such gorgeous locks," Doc adds, reaching out and stroking my dark brown hair. I slap his hand off just as Mom walks up to us.

"Thanks so much for coming, Docky." Ugh. Docky. Really? Doc is cheesy enough, but *Docky*?

"Good evening, Brandi, my darling," Marvin says, kissing the back of her hand.

Doc's Euro-trashy eyes trace my mom's fit little body—from her black-and-white referee top, to the pleated black miniskirt, to the black spiked heels. He should get a twenty-yard penalty for perviness.

"I was just getting to know Emery a little bit better," Doc says, his eyes back above her neck. "I was about to tell her that I can relate to her. My sister struggled with her weight as a teenager. I know how restrictive it can be."

I shoot eye darts at my mom.

"Have you told Emery about the show?" Mom asks.

"Well, no, but we were getting to that." Marvin turns to me. "Emery, your darling mother here told me about your brand audit meeting last night."

This is the part of the conversation where Doc concedes defeat, shakes my hand, and thanks me for my time before moving on to the next lame show idea his production company is cooking up starring some sad-sack group of desperate people. Then Mom gets back to obsessing over trying desperately to keep my dad attracted to her aging face and body, Angel's career, and hiding food from me, and then I go and slip my duck-face mask back on and get more of those chocolate doughnuts I just saw on the tray on the coffee table.

"Oh, yeah, the brand audit meeting," I say. "Amazing stuff. Brilliant. I loved it."

"So I've heard," Doc says. "And I found your candor quite inspiring. It takes a big person to be that honest."

"No pun intended," I say.

"That's not what I mean, Emery." Doc takes a swig of his beer. "Not at all. In fact, I think a lot of people wish they could be more like you."

"Fat like me?"

"No, *honest* like you." He empties the remnants of beer down his throat and exhales. "You're a star, Emery. A natural, made-for-TV star. And I have finally—after consulting with some network execs—come up with the perfect show for your family. But to be totally honest, this is a show that we positively cannot do without you."

"What show could I possibly star in? *The Biggest Loser*?"

"Actually . . ." Marvin combs his black-and-gray speckled beard with his sausage-link fingers. "It would be a documentary-style series about you trying to lose some weight. Tastefully done, of course."

"Yeah, Emery," Mom eagerly adds. "It would be classy. Not trashy at all. It will, um, like help people."

I've never heard the words "classy" and reality TV put in the same sentence, but then again I have never been cornered at a Halloween party by two middle-aged adults, with one dressed as a pot-bellied pirate and the other a trashy ref.

"I have done everything humanly possible to lose weight, so it's not gonna happen," I say. "Trainers, nutritionists, a fat camp in Malibu. I have cut down to two Double Western Bacons a week. I don't think this show would work. Sorry. I'm sure you can find someone else."

"But we would supply the best team in the business," Marvin says. "The same one that turned Taylor Alison into a trim goddess."

"But Taylor Alison has always been skinny."

"Actually, she did have some, shall we say, 'loose' areas," he counters, as Mom nods with affirmation. "Everyone has room for improvement. Even pop stars."

These people are demented, and clearly I'm being ambushed. Am I being punk'd? I look around the room for cameras. I don't see any. *Where's Ben to save me?*

"So is this an intervention or something?" I ask. "Seriously, I can't believe you guys would—"

Mom awkwardly drapes her arm around me. She turns her back to Doc and whispers to me, "Honey, this is not an intervention. This is simply an *opportunity*. You just have to trust me on this. Your father and sister are a hundred percent behind this. It is a win-win for all of us. It broke my heart to see that sad look on your face the other day at the costume shop. I saw you looking at all those sexy outfits wishing you could fit into them."

"But I wanted to be Duck Face. You know that."

Okay, fine, she's right. But I'm not about to admit it in front of this British pound cake.

"Fine, Mom. But why should I trust *him*?" I crane my neck so my head points at Marvin. Or Doc. Or whatever the heck he's called. "I mean, he makes people eat bugs and sleep with strangers so they can win a Jeep Cherokee. And he goes by 'Doc' even though he's never even graduated from college."

"This would be a much different show than I have previously done, my dear," Marvin explains. "Uplifting. Inspirational. *Aspirational.* America loves a feel-good story . . . and so do advertisers, I might add."

"You'd be the ugly duckling transforming into a beautiful swan," Mom adds.

I give her my best Disgusted Daughter Face.

Marvin and Mom stand staring at me like they're the last two finalists and I'm Ryan Seacrest about to announce the winner.

"Let me think about it." I grab Marvin by the wrist and peek at his shiny silver Rolex and silently count off two seconds. "Okay," I abruptly announce. "I've come to my decision: not a chance."

Mom looks over at Doc. When he nods a yes to her, Mom leans in toward my ear and adds, "Honey, but what if they paid us a million dollars?"

TUESDAY, NOVEMBER 5

Ben and I hooked up at the Halloween party.

After my mom attempted to prostitute me out to Doc so she could get her stupid reality show, I immediately went and found Ben. I grabbed him by the hand and we lurked upstairs to my bedroom, where I locked the door and got down to business. The first thing I did: turned off the lights. And then I closed the blinds, just in case a sliver of moonlight should find its way inside and illuminate my fleshy whiteness.

"Get over here, Em," Ben said, standing by my bed. Or at least I assume he was, given I couldn't see more than two inches in front of my face. Either way, he knew what he was in for, and judging from the few dozen other times we have done the deed, he rather liked to do this.

"Are you blind as a bat? I am right here, Ben."

"Where?"

Still in costume, I knelt down and poked the nose of my silly duck-face mask above his crotch and squawked, "Quack, quack!"

"Maybe if it wasn't so dark in here I could see you," Ben said, lifting me up by my armpits and kissing me.

"You don't want to see me. Trust me."

"But I do." Ben cupped my cheeks in his hands and started kissing me like I was a supermodel. "Just shut up."

As Ben's big hands worked their way down along my big sides, my big shoulders tightened up as he squeezed a roll of big mush on my hips. He turned me on as he always does, the big lug.

Here's the thing about sex and Big Girls: Just because we might look like someone you would never, ever want to have sex with doesn't mean that we, ourselves, don't want to have sex. We are still human, after all. We have hormones. We have urges. We have our needs. The biggest difference might be we just prefer to do it with the lights off.

It's nice to be touched, to be adored . . . even if with every squeeze I am reminded of how much bigger I have gotten over the last year or so. The annoyance of my mom and Doc's tacky proposal was still on my mind, and I pulled back from Ben mid-makeout.

"Why are you even attracted to me?" I asked, thinking I would slap him if he said my "personality" or my "face."

"I don't know," he replied, his hands sliding down to my butt, which was, by the way, wedged into black *streeeeetch* cotton pants. "You're just irresistible to me. I love you."

Wow, love really is blind. Like, really, really, really blind.

But just to be safe, I still kept the lights off.

Now it's a week after Halloween, and I still haven't forgiven my mom for ambushing me at the party. And seeing as though I have been giving her the silent treatment ever since, I'd imagine she knows as much. But she hasn't said a word about it. I know that can't last for long.

This isn't the first time Mom has bribed me to lose weight. She has offered me Gucci purses, trips to Disneyland, a cruise through the Caribbean to swim with manatees, and thousand-dollar shopping sprees. Suggesting I could get a million dollars for losing weight on a reality show is a first for her, but the over-all obnoxiousness of her bribing is not.

When I walk through the front door after school, I see Mom in the living room doing squats while holding a red rubber exer-cise ball in each hand as she watches an exercise video. I can practically see strands of muscle bulging inside her tights. Why Dad doesn't ever just sit and watch her exercise, what with her firm body and all, is a good question. In fact, the only thing more MIA than Dad lately is my ability to avoid eating after nine o'clock at night.

"Eight, nine, and . . . ten." She's panting. "Hi, Em. Almost done." She wipes the sweat from her forehead with the sleeve of her right forearm.

"Nice balls," I say brightly.

I walk past her and head upstairs. Yet again, she doesn't talk about It. Nor does she suggest I join her Buns of Iron work-out session.

Maybe Mom has moved on from the whole reality TV thinga-majig. I haven't even heard her mention Doc's name in over a week. Perhaps evolution is not dead, after all.

Entering my room, I crash onto my bed face first, smushing my face into the pillow. I'm bored. And tired. And hungry. Energy, that's it! Energy is what I need.

A few minutes later, I muster enough to get up and mope over to my distressed-wood dresser and open the top underwear drawer. I fish through my jumble of granny panties and reach into the back and grope around until I find what it is I am looking for: a milky chocolate bar, which I had stuffed away for a rainy day like this. Or one that is seventy-eight and sunny.

I tear open the foil wrapper with my teeth and peel it open like a banana. But unlike a banana, the bar melts scrumptiously in my mouth as I reflexively moan.

Knock, knock, knock.

"Emery? Almost ready?"

Ugh. Why didn't I lock the door? I stuff the wrapper into the drawer and slam it shut.

"Oh yes," I say calmly. "Just getting changed is all."

"Meet me in the car in two minutes."

That was a close call. I had promised Mom, Dad, and Dr. Hung that I would no longer smuggle sugary treats into my bedroom. It was a pact that I even pinky sweared to uphold after my family's most recent Obesity Intervention, during which I confessed to sneaking bad-for-you foods into my room.

Step number one is admitting you have a problem.

I sit on the edge of my bed and tug off my size sixteen black jeggings, wiggling out one snug-fitting pant leg at a time. While I commend Macy's for offering "skinny" style "comfort" jeans for fatties like me, in reality they should have consulted with a physicist first.

After burning off half my candy bar just squeezing out of my jeans, I slip on a pair of far more cozy, lightweight cotton sweats and a purple T-shirt that is baggy enough to conceal a few sacks of potatoes.

A few minutes later, I plop into the passenger's seat of Mom's car and we're off to beach volleyball.

"Ben's meeting us there, right?" Mom asks, pulling backward out of the driveway.

"Yes," I say.

"And is he bringing his balls?"

I giggle. "That's a very personal question."

"Oh, Em." An anxiety exhale. Followed by another one. "Are you ever going to outgrow this sense of humor?"

Mom guides our black Prius down the steep incline of the street that drops down to the beach. Over the summer, I had promised my parents I would partake in an after-school athletic activity at least twice a week. It was a deal I made with them in exchange for a two-week vacation with Ben and his family to Florida back in July. His grandparents are retired there, living in a small town a couple hours' drive north of Tampa called Crystal River. The town, with a population of 3,000 people, sits right on the Gulf of Mexico. Its small-town charm is something right out of a Nicholas Sparks novel.

For as long as I have known Ben (since middle school), he has been telling me all about his summers in Crystal River. His grandparents live right on a manatee sanctuary. Manatees, in case you have never watched Animal Planet and don't know about them, are an endangered species that live in the waters around Florida and the Caribbean. They're known as "the cows of the sea" because they each weigh like a thousand pounds and basically just float around and lazily eat sea grass all day.

Unfortunately, the massive size of the manatee, combined with their tragic inability to swim fast, makes them vulnerable to getting cut by the motors of redneck boaters speeding through their grazing areas. This led to the government designating certain waterways as protected, where manatees could swim without worrying about boats cutting them up. And Crystal River is one of these safe havens.

In California, Ben always seems stressed out about something. School, his parents pressuring him to work, getting good grades, missing out on fun stuff at school. Weighing close to three hundred pounds, yet having no interest in football or contact sports of any kind, Ben doesn't fit into the mainstream life of Highland. But in Crystal River, he seemed free.

Every morning on our vacation (besides the one when a thunderstorm exploded on us), we would get up before the tourist divers came into the sanctuary behind his grandparents' house and we'd swim alongside the manatees in the warm, spring-fed, crystal-clear waters. For being so ginormous, manatees are gentle, trusting creatures. Unlike the spastic dolphins, freak-me-out sharks, and cagey seals off the coast of Highland Beach, the manatees would float along the bottom and let us rub their backs or feed them grass as if they were our pets.

It was during that vacation to Crystal River that I decided I wanted to become a marine biologist; it was also when I decided that I had fallen in love with Ben, mostly for introducing me to creatures who were chubby, slow, and plodding, yet elegant and graceful and kind. And they were happy. Content. Free from worry—except for finding a quiet place to nap along the bottom.

They didn't partake in feeding frenzies with sharks. They didn't feel the need to cruise the depths of the Gulf of Mexico with the whales. Instead, the manatees enjoyed just . . . being. And in Florida last summer, so did Ben and I.

I don't complain when Mom drops me off at the pier and says she will be back in an hour and a half. I am not a fan of beach volleyball. In fact, I really hate it. I simply suck at it, and next to lawn bowling, it has to be one of the most boring sports. Standing in sand, especially the deep sand of Highland where it is hard to even walk, let alone dodge and sprint about for volleyballs in the hot sun, while gawkers watch you from the bike path, is not at all my idea of fun. Add to it the fact that almost everyone else playing looks like a swimsuit model.

But it beats soccer (too much running), basketball (also too much running), hockey (I'm a pacifist), and swimming. (Me in a swimsuit? Ain't gonna happen, kids!) So by process of elimination, and due to the fact that Dad spent many hours of my youth teaching me and Angel how to play, my sports effort has come to this silly game in sand.

"Your hair looks cute," Ben says before hugging me while the other players warm up by the nets. "Love the ponytail." His puffy cheeks blow up like balloons when he smiles.

If I were modest, I would blush. But since I am not, I just say, "I try, I try."

The after-school program is run by the city, which means we play by "Highland rules"—"six-man" with three blockers and hitters in the front row by the net and three in the row behind. The first team to get twenty-five points wins.

I take the back row (because I have a vertical leap of about an inch) and we start the first game. Six weeks into the season and we have won a grand total of zero games, which may have something to do with the fact that Ben and I royally suck at volleyball.

Today we are playing a group of kids from Lawrence, the town just east of Highland. They aren't exactly fans of ours. They think we are the rich, snooty kids who live near the beach, while they are the working-class stiffs from an inland suburb. The stereotypes are sort of true, but because I live on the east side of Coastal Highway, far from the beach, I feel like I am more like the Lawrence kids. They don't see it that way, however.

"Serve it up, brat," a greasy-haired boy in board shorts barks at me from the other side of the net. Their three boy players are all playing without shirts, just like the pros. Their three girls, meanwhile, are wearing bikinis. My team? Our bodies are so covered up we look like we are dressed for an ice hockey game.

I toss the white ball up and boink at it with an underhand serve. It arcs about ten feet and lands a few feet short of the net. Point, Inlanders.

"Nice serve, Kerri Walsh," a tall boy trash-talks from the front row.

"Yeah, Kerri Walsh times a hundred." A muscular kid with eyes too small for his face chuckles.

I ignore them. One of my teammates, a sweet-faced if unathletic girl in thick glasses named Peggy whose dad makes her play sports even though she's blinder than a bat, rolls the ball over to the bad guys' side for their serve.

Tiny-Eyed Troll tosses it high above his head, leaps into the air, and with a windmill motion, strikes the ball like a bullet over the net. I dive forward to save it, but the ball bounces a few feet in front of my outstretched hands. I face-plant and come up with a mouth full of California's finest sedimentary sand.

Ben comes running over as I stand doubled-over yakking like a TB patient.

"You okay, Em?" he says.

Coughing. Hacking. Dry spitting.

"Here, have some water," Ben offers, handing me a plastic bottle.

The other team's players stand impatiently with their hands on their hips as I swig and spit like I'm at the dentist.

I'm able to get enough crunchy pebbles out of my mouth to return to the game, but by then I am too shaken up to help my team very much.

A half hour later, it's game point and we are down 24–2. I'm sweating like a pig. Wearing black cotton sweatpants and a T-shirt on the beach playing volleyball will do that to a person. I just want the stupid game to end. If Ben wasn't so intent on showing those Lawrence losers that we aren't quitters, I would have pretended I needed to take a bathroom break and left already.

The other team serves and Ben is able to bump it back over the net into the hands of one of their front three, who sets it for a lanky kid who winds up and hits the ball straight down. Ben leaps up to block it, but his arms are too far apart and the ball bullets between his wrists and strikes him smack in the face. From the back row, I can see the blood gushing from his nose before he even plops onto his knees, pressing his hand against it in an attempt to stop the bleeding.

"Sorry, bro," the hitter says sarcastically before high-fiving his teammates.

Game over.

I do my best to play nurse, handing Ben a beach towel and rubbing his back. A few minutes later, both teams have left the beach and it's just Ben and me sitting there.

The bleeding eventually stops and Ben, staring out at the ocean with the saddest face I have ever seen on him, says, "You should do the reality show."

"What?"

"That show your mom wants to do. I think you should do it."

"I can't believe you, of all people, would want me to do that show."

"Maybe some good will come out of it. Maybe you and I could use the money to move to Florida. Maybe we could open that manatee tour boat company we talked about. Think about the big picture."

"But, Ben, we talked about this. Everyone who ends up on a reality show ends up being a pathetic joke."

"You mean, a joke like this?" He points to his swollen face. "If my arms weren't so fat I could have blocked that hit. I'm already a joke, Emery."

"Being heavy doesn't mean you're a joke. Unless you can laugh at it, which is what I do."

"But maybe you shouldn't make a joke out of everything, Em. Maybe your doctor has a point. Maybe it's time for us to be healthier. I'm tired of all this."

"So you're tired of me?"

"No, not at all," he says. "And stop putting words in my mouth. I'm just tired of not being *normal*. And like it or not, Em, we are not normal. We are like lepers around here. Around anywhere."

"We'd be skinny in, like, West Virginia," I reason.

"You think if you make fun of yourself that it makes it okay. But it doesn't."

"Okay, Bennigan, so let me get this straight." I brush off the sand from my pants as I stand up. "You think going on a reality show will make me more normal? Have you seen reality TV shows lately? I have three words for you: Honey Boo Boo."

I turn on my heel and stomp off toward the pier. This isn't the boy who has always loved me unconditionally, making me feel wanted in a loving way. This isn't the first and only boy who has ever touched me, held me, made me feel sexy. This is just another ant marching along the line of conformity that is making our society so freaking lame.

Ben chases after me, stumbling in the sand like a drunk on New Year's. "C'mon, Em. Hold on, now—"

"I can't have this conversation with you." I stop and push him back, and in so doing, I slip. With my legs rubbery from the exertion of traipsing across this ridiculously long beach, I collapse into a heap, banging my head on Ben's knee on the way down. Which, of course, causes Ben to fall back in pain and whimper like a kicked puppy. And there we lie, like two pathetic beached whales. I begin with a laugh, but soon I start crying.

"I'm sorry," Ben says, rolling on top of me and hugging me till I can barely breathe. I push him off so I can get some oxygen.

"Don't apologize for saying what you believe," I say, "because that's less respectable than the ignorant point you're making in the first place."

"I shouldn't be dumping my issues on you," he explains. "I'm the one who looked like a fool out there on the court. This is exactly why I don't play sports. It just brings out the worst in people."

"No," I tell him. "What brings out the worst in people are the lies we are told. The ads in magazines with anorexic, airbrushed models who make girls develop distorted self images and think they aren't beautiful because they don't look like them, even though what the models look like is a total lie. And the lies that our parents tell us when we are little. Like when I was eleven, and had a belly so big the kids started calling me 'Buddha.' You know what my mom told me? She told me people with big hearts have big bellies. That's total lying parent bullshit. When you have a belly as big as mine, your heart isn't big. It's broken."

Ben stares into my eyes. "Oh, Emery." He wraps his arms around my lower back, pulling me close to him. "I just can't stand to see you feeling heartbroken."

"Who said I was heartbroken?"

"You just did."

WEDNESDAY, NOVEMBER 6

"You know what I love the most?" Angel asks from the backseat as I drive. "Like more than anything ever?"

"Makeup?" I guess.

"Um, no, Emery!" she huffs. "I mean, I do love makeup, but even more than makeup."

"I have no clue. What do you love the most, Angel?"

"I love not camping. I really love *not* camping."

"You realize that's a totally ridiculous statement."

"No, I don't, actually," she says.

I grip the wheel tighter. "You can't say the thing you love the most in all the world is *not* doing something. You could, for example, say, 'I love staying in swag hotels,' or 'I really love the comfort of sleeping under an actual roof in a building with heat and a Wi-Fi connection.' But you can't say that, more than anything else, you love *not camping*. And I'm telling you this as someone who thinks camping should only be experienced by people from the 1800s and the homeless."

"Emery," she sneers. "Who made you the judge and jury?"

"Dad."

"How could Dad possibly be okay with this?"

"Well, since Dad is hardly ever home anymore, someone in this family has to step up and be the *de facto* voice of reason."

"Emery"—Mom suddenly butts in from the passenger's seat—"you're larger, but, really, you shouldn't call yourself a fatso."

"I said 'de facto,' Mom."

"Or that," Mom replies. "Whatever. Just everyone stop bickering and let's get back to talking about our show. Since Emery doesn't want to do Doc's idea, we need another concept."

Mom starts chewing her fingernails and spitting them onto the floor mat.

"You're better at this *thinking stuff* than I am," she adds. "Please, help me brainstorm here!"

I'm more worried about focusing right now on learning how to drive without crashing, but to appease Mom, not to mention to distract me from Angel bugging the crap out of me (per the norm of my life), I pretend to ponder her query. I even scratch my head and let out a pensive-ish "*hmmm*" before quickly returning my left and right hands to ten and two o'clock on the wheel (Mom hates when I drive with one hand "like a rapper," though she can't even name a single one). I even throw in another "*hmmm*" for good measure.

I am not really thinking of stupid reality show ideas for her. I am, however, thinking about how hungry I am and whether or not I will have chicken nuggets or a burger for lunch . . . or perhaps both. Decisions, decisions. Ah, screw it. I'll make this easy and just have pizza. Deep dish. Extra cheese.

"Doc says that to get your own show these days, you really need a killer concept," she says, nibbling a sliver of skin from the cuticle of her right thumb.

Farther down the road, she picks off a white fleck of residual cuticle from her injectable-enhanced bottom lip and flicks it out the passenger's side window.

I shrug and keep driving, hoping she will move on to a far less self-indulgent topic than reality TV superstardom, which is little more than a fame-seeking plan for my older sister that—get ready for it—I WANT NOTHING TO DO WITH! Because, you know, these days everyone is doing it! It's the iPhone generation's even more narcissistic version of keeping up with the Joneses.

"I'm talking about, like, something no one has ever seen before. Something . . ." Mom gazes through the windshield of our Toyota in deep thought as if she will find inspiration from the BMW in front of us. "Something . . ."

"Different?" I offer.

"Yes!" she squeals. "Different! Something totally *different*."

At this point, what I really want to do is tell Mom she should expand her vocabulary to include grown-up words like "different." This might actually prove a more achievable goal than creating an original concept for a show that already hasn't been done a hundred times. I also want to artfully suggest that surviving on a diet of coffee, water, Adderall, Ambien, Xanax, Klonopin, and protein-rich smoothies so that she can stay a size two could be just what's disabling her calorie-deprived brain.

This not being an ideal world, however, I don't have the heart to burst her bliss bubble. At least she's letting me drive today, a task that has been left mostly to Dad ever since a near-miss with a careless cat last month.

"Doc told me that our family could be The Next Big Thing," she says, fashioning air quotes with her fingers around "thing."

As Doc sees it, we've got a great "cast":

- "The Dad": Jasper Jackson, who has gone from being a pro basketball player to an athletic trainer/motivational speaker/absentee father;

- "The Mom": Brandi Jackson, a former actress/cheerleader and current Momager; a Real Housewife of Highland Beach;

- "The Perfect Daughter": Angel, a senior and self-absorbed cheerleader whom Mom is intent on turning into America's next top TV actress/hostess/model/Bikini Girl in *Maxim*;

And last, but certainly not least . . .

- "Angel's Wisecracking Chubby Sister": Me, featuring a world-class wit, unmatched teenage precociousness, disdain for cheerleaders and obnoxiously skinny people, and a waistline as big as my personality.

Doc apparently has even come up with a show title—"The Jackson Four"—but he warned my mom that he hadn't yet sprinkled his "genius dust" onto the project and fleshed out a "killer" concept. The pedestal on which Mom places "Doc" is so high you'd think the guy is an actual doctor and not a ~~former~~ failed filmmaker named Marvin.

I can see how a housewife would find the fortysomething Doc, who has never been married, semi-handsome—you know, "the kind of guy who will roofie you" definition of handsome. I don't take seriously my creeping fear that she wants to do Doc. He is unpleasantly plump, round in the middle, and walks with a limp shuffle that makes him appear about as athletic as, well, me.

"Whoa!" Mom yelps. "Be CAREFUL!"

Ever the dutiful daughter (cough, cough), I come to a tire-screeching halt at the edge of the intersection, sending Mom doubling over her seat belt.

"Don't brake so hard, Emery!" Her silver hoop earrings are swaying like porch wind chimes. "Make it more gradual. Yeesh."

"Emery, you're gonna kill us," Angel snarls in from the backseat, just when I had almost forgotten she was there.

Mom flips down the visor mirror and checks her Perma-dyed blonde hair (and her forehead wrinkles while she's at it), already apparently forgetting that I almost just killed all three of us and destroyed our Prius. "Be careful. The last thing we can afford is *another* accident."

THURSDAY, NOVEMBER 7

It's just past midnight and I've had enough homework. So over it. I don't really care to know that Jefferson and Washington both advocated for a smaller government and write a two-page essay on what political party they would most connect with today. Especially when my stomach is barking like a dog.

I close my laptop and head down to the kitchen for a snack. Dad tells me people should eat six meals a day. Granted, they're supposed to be "small" meals and you aren't supposed to eat after 7:00 p.m. But I am not good at math—or at not eating when my body is telling me to put food in my face.

I lurk down the hardwood steps slowly, quietly. There are two floorboards—the third and fourth from the bottom to be exact—that creak like a haunted house. But I'm a veteran prowler. I know that I can step on the far side of each and avoid the creaky parts, thus allowing me to slip down for a snack without the shame or judgment of the three other sleepers in the house.

Safely downstairs, I walk into the pantry and grab a loaf of
bread, a jar of peanut butter, and a box of cornflakes and walk
out, arms full. After popping four slices into the toaster, I tick-
tock tap my fingers waiting for the bread to turn golden brown
and start thumbing through the mail that is stacked in a neat
pile on the brown granite counter. I find:

- A reminder card from the dentist for Angel to get her bimonthly teeth
  whitening;

- The gas bill;

- A catalog of useless preppy clothes that don't come in anything over a size
  twelve and thus I will never shop from;

- The electric bill;

- The cable bill;

- Copy of the *Beach Cities Weekly* newspaper; and

- A letter folded in half.

I unfold and open the letter, look around to make sure no
one is around, and read it:

1115 Ocean Avenue
Highland Beach, California 90266

Dear Mr. and Mrs. Jackson:

This letter is a formal notification that you are in default of your
obligation to make several payments on your home loan, account
#4203303. This current account holds the sum of $498,000,
payable by March 15.

The outstanding amount has been overdue since June 15 and
you have ignored multiple requests to make a payment or recon-
solidate your debt.

Unless the full amount is received between now and the above deadline (March 15), we will have no choice but to begin the fore-closure process on your home. We have given you more than adequate notice on this issue, and we have no other choice.

Please act accordingly,

Beach Cities Lending Inc.

Before I can process what a colossal cluster this bank let-ter might mean for my family, my toast pops up. I proceed to lather on a thick layer of peanut butter on all four slices of toast. Make that, extra-extra peanut butter. I carefully coat the edges around each side to the crust, then lick clean the silver butter knife.

I reach for the plastic bear-shaped bottle and squirt a smiley face of honey on each piece of bread. As I press the slices together to make two gooey sandwiches, my mouth is salivating.

After sitting at the counter scarfing down Mount Emery (as an unsolicited public service, Mom once notified me this favorite late-night toasty snack totals 600–800 calories), I dump corn-flakes into my favorite white bowl and douse it with soy milk[4], then top my creation with a few spoonfuls of sugar. I eat quickly, before they lose their crunch.

Fluffer Nutter (don't ask, but, yes, it is a boy), our family's eleven-year-old white Pomeranian, is now standing at my feet, panting for scraps. I let him lick the bowl. Fluffy gets special treatment. He is, after all, the one creature in this house who doesn't judge me for my binge eating and simply wants to join in on the fun.

After letting Fluffer also lick my plate clean, I quietly walk

---

[4] Lactose makes me bloaty and farty.

upstairs and by midnight I'm in my bed and staring at the ceiling. I'm now so full I can barely manage the strength to pick up the remote control off my nightstand.

I'm all caught up on my Netflix shows. So I flick on the flat-screen TV and start surfing. *Conan* has a boring actor talking about how "amazing" her hunky male costar is in the schlocky movie she's promoting. MTV has a rerun of *Jersey Shore* I've seen like a hundred times. ABC Family is airing some boring soap. Somewhere up in the 400s I stop on an infomercial hosted by an absurdly athletic-looking lady named Jessica LaClair. She calls herself "a different kind of body transformer."

I usually surf past these idiotic infomercials. If anything, it is sort of an act of defiance for being forced to sit through my mom's commercial-watching marathons throughout my childhood.

But there's something about Jessica that is different. Although she is wearing tight black shorts and a jogging bra, nothing on her body is jiggling as she leaps down a flight of stairs and does a flip onto a sidewalk, urging everyone to "get off the couch if you want to lose that pouch. Pouches are for kangaroos, ladies!"

"I used to look like this," she later declares confidently into the camera. A photo of a chunky version of her standing sad-faced with more rolls than an Italian bakery flashes on the screen. "But now I look like this!"

Then a pic appears on the right side of the screen showing her svelte and tan and flexing her biceps. She looks like an entirely different person except for her face.

She is so pretty that I have to press Pause and stare at it. In her "before" shot, she has rosy red chipmunk chubby cheeks that frame her round doe eyes. Her skin is lavatory sink white and clear, near flawless. Her face is all cheekbones and delicate chin. But as I scan down her body, draped in unflattering white shorts and a too-tight T-shirt clinging to her round midsection, I can see that she was a "pretty face" girl—just as I am now.

And for the first time in a long while, I feel like I. Don't. Want. To. Be. Me.

I mean, on the outside. I am perfectly fine with the specimen inside. But in the quiet of my bedroom, with just me and Jessica flexing in front of me and her blonde ponytail bouncing cutely, I feel an ounce of motivation to—maybe, possibly, perhaps—finally do something about my weight.

I press Play on the DVR and Jessica's infomercial launches back into motion.

A flurry of quick-cut shots. Hopping onto and off a park bench. Climbing atop a fence and flipping forward like an acrobat, landing on the grass and rolling into a ball like a stuntman. Leaping over a picnic table.

"This is not your mother's exercise program," she explains. "Freerunning is the only form of exercise that you can do simply by stepping out of your front door. Who needs the gym when you have the world outside? Freerunning is the art of expressing yourself in your environment without limitations: Inspired by Parkour, the French military's obstacle training, freerunning is the art of movement and action. It combines acrobatics, gymnastics, and old-fashioned play. And if you buy my video, you can learn how to make it the art of your own *physical freedom*. You will transform your body from this"—on flashes yet another doughy fat-girl photo—"to this!" Her toned bod of today comes on.

Jessica isn't a skinny bitch. She doesn't have the kind of Barbie body like my sister, which I will never have. She is built solidly, with strong, thick thighs and broad shoulders. I could see doing what she does. That is, if I wasn't too lazy to even lift my head off this pillow and turn off the lamp that sits just outside the reach of my plump right arm.

What Jessica is doing actually looks like fun. It looks like it is some sort of edgy, fringe sport that uses the outdoors as a playground. Stairs, curbs, benches, fences, chairs, cars, signs, light poles, walls, ledges.

Sports suck. So do gyms. Gyms give me the creeps. All those self-absorbed jock types and mirrors covering every wall. It's a fat person's worst nightmare come to life in a fluorescent box of body-obsessed tools.

So the idea of doing freerunning out in the wild, now that would be something I would actually consider doing. Maybe, possibly. It looks like fun and technically, anything fun cannot be called exercise. The idea of experiencing the sensation of flight—albeit momentarily—is pretty cool. I mean, more than being skinny. More than being rich. More than famous. Being able to *fly* still remains the ultimate representation of human freedom.

"We all are born with the desire to feel free," Jessica explains. "The ultimate sensation of physical freedom is flying. With freerunning, you can experience a moment of flight. And once you do, you will become addicted to the feeling. And you will change your life."

A phone number to call for the video, *True Freedom*, pops on the screen and as I'm actually considering freezing the frame so

I can make history and order my first-ever exercise video, the TV screen goes blank. Just black, but the blue power light on the front of the TV frame is still on. Odd. I didn't even press a button on the remote yet. In today's day and age, technological things aren't supposed to malfunction. In fact, there are three fundamental rules of modern life:

1) You're lame if you don't own a laptop.

2) God created "smartphones" so we no longer have to talk to humans.

3) Gadgets aren't supposed to break.

Groaning, I sit up, point the remote directly at the TV and press down hard on the power button, but the TV just turns off. So I turn it back on again. The screen, however, stays black. I roll out of bed and walk over to the TV and check the cable connection. It's stuck in the back slot as always.

Troubleshooting TV tech troubles being way below my pay scale, I shuffle back to bed and drop back down on the mattress. Soon I fall into a deep sleep featuring dreams of a simpler time in America when we could all sit in the peaceful solitude of our bedrooms and do something people could do in the 1950s: WATCH A DAMN TV!

FRIDAY, NOVEMBER 8

To say that most mornings I am "grumpy" would be an All-Star caliber understatement that could qualify me to play competitively in the NUL.[5] In fact, it's an understatement that ranks right up there with the following understatements:

- Angel really is not very smart.

- Mom overuses Botox and thus has fewer forehead lines than a toddler.

- Dad barely looks at Mom anymore no matter how much she Botoxes.

- I would die without any food for more than three hours.

- Highland High School lunches need larger portions.

- Marvin Harris is an old perv.

So when I stumble downstairs for breakfast and hear Mom and Angel chirping like shiny, happy people chattering in the kitchen about their usual pointlessness—*That is such an*

---

[5] National Understatement League . . . but don't bother Googling it (I made it up).

adorable blouse. . . . Yes, Lauren is a total gossip. . . . I actually think they look more real when they're fake. . . .—I'm regretting not wishing for the power to make myself deaf the last time I saw a shooting star.

"Good morning, *Emeryyyyyyy*!" Mom perks. "I made you girls some egg whites with avocado and tomato."

"So yummy," Angel says.

"I know, right?" Mom agrees, handing me a plate. "Give it a try, Em."

I sit down at the kitchen counter and begin "eating" her anorexic food. That's when I notice the letter, the one from the bank, is sitting on the counter next to the plate where I left it last night.

"What's wrong with this freakin' remote?" Angel grumbles. "It's broken or something."

Angel hands it to Mom like it's a piece of toxic waste. "Like, seriously," Angel complains.

Mom picks open the battery cover with her thick polished fingernail and twists the AAs around. She points it at the tiny TV perched on the far end of the counter and nothing happens.

"Try the computer," I offer. "See if that's working. You know, maybe the cable is messed up."

Angel flips open Mom's laptop on the dining room table and pounds at the Return key like it is her bitch. "This piece of crap won't work either," she whines.

"Huh, must be an outage," Mom says.

"Or maybe you didn't pay the cable bill," I say, raising an eyebrow.

Mom glares back at me. I don't respond. I just look down at the bank foreclosure letter and look back at her again. I do this three times before she gets the hint.

By now, Angel has gone to the bathroom to change into her workout clothes for the gym. It's just us.

"I saw the letter," I begin.

"Okay," she says.

"Why didn't you tell us it was this bad?"

"Because I didn't know it was this bad. Your dad handles the finances, Emmy."

"That's a load of crap. You knew. How did it get this bad? I thought his business had just slowed down? I didn't realize it was this big of a mess!"

"Something about bad investments, some upside-down real estate deals. You'd have to ask your father, because I really don't know."

"I would ask him if he was ever here anymore."

"Well," Mom says with a sigh, "he's got to travel because he's got to go where the business is, where there is money to be made. The Midwest."

"Money. Like what you get from going on a reality TV show?" I ask.

Mom pours a cup of coffee into the *Today* mug Dad gave her last year after he appeared on the show as a Life Expert. This black coffee is her breakfast.

"Emery," she says. "A reality show would make a difference."

"The difference between what? Being homeless or not?"

Mom sips from her mug and licks her lips. She looks old in the morning, bags under her eyes. I almost feel bad for her. Almost.

"Yes," she says. "If you are asking if we really could use that million dollars, the answer is yes."

WEDNESDAY, NOVEMBER 13

"Why did you name me Emery?" I asked my mom one day as she did yoga in the bedroom on her favorite purple mat.

It's a natural question a child asks their parents at some point. If you're really precocious, it happens when you are around three, which is how old I was when I popped the question. My best friend at the time, Tori, had told me her parents named her after an actress on some show called *Beverly Hills, 90210*.

"Am I named after a TV character?" I asked her.

"No, no, no, no, dear. I would never do something so tacky as that." Mom had always thought Tori's parents, with their expensive everything and flashy this and that, were "trashy." Naming your child after Tori Spelling was just extra cheese on the cheesecake.

"I will never forget how it happened," she continued. "I was at the nail salon when I was eight months pregnant and hadn't thought of a name for you yet. I mean, it was a crazy time. Your dad was in the playoffs for the NBA championship and there I was, all roly-poly at every game. I had to look my best. You know, for the cameras and fans and all. So I am at the salon and I hear the nail tech shout to another tech across the salon, 'Can you toss me an emery board?' And it was like, 'That's it!' I knew I would name you Emery."

Why Mom thinks being named after a piece of cardboard is classier than being named after a '90s TV star is anyone's guess. I also wonder if she knew something about the beast stirring within her womb. I mean, emery boards are abrasive, rough, the opposite of silky and smooth.

"Why did you call Angel 'Angel'?"

Mom thought about it for a second. Then she picked me up by my lumpy toddler torso, stared straight into my brown eyes and said, "Because, Emery, your sister was simply an angel sent from above."

I'm recounting this lovely childhood story in front of a group of strangers while sitting in a conference room on the ninth floor of a concrete box in the middle of Beverly Hills, where I had sucked up every last bit of pride and agreed to take a meeting with the brass at THE NETWORK. This is the cable network where Doc supposedly has something called a "first-look deal" in which he has to pitch them all his shows before anywhere else.

When Doc and I were sitting in uncomfortably modern couches in the sleek lobby, an assistant girl came down to meet us and handed me a questionnaire on a clipboard. "The team would like you to fill this out," the perky twentysomething said.

The questions weren't exactly the stuff of an AP exam. In addition to the usual age, hometown, and names of family members were questions like . . .

Who's your best friend? My iPhone.

Do you have a boyfriend? Yes, his name is Ben.

Is there any part of your life you wouldn't want to appear on camera? Pretty much anything occurring in a bathroom.

Why do you want to be on a reality show? Who said I did?

Who is your hero? It's a tie between Jenna Marbles and David Hasselhoff, circa 1991.

What reality star would you most want to be like? None. They're all pretty sad, lame people.

What sports do you like? None, but I did recently see an infomercial for a cool activity called "Freerunning." I'd try that.

Who is your favorite celebrity? I don't like celebrities enough to have a favorite.

Who is your favorite singer? Not Taylor Swift. Her whole sense of self-worth seems to be wrapped up in what guys think of her. Bad message. Pitbull seems cool. Miley isn't afraid to let her freak flag fly. Me likey.

What is your favorite movie? *Waiting for Guffman* and *American Movie*. Irony is not dead!

What's your favorite animal? The manatee. But it's a mammal. Technically.

What occupation do you aspire to? Besides "Freelance Couch Surfer," I'd like to be a marine biologist because then I can hang out with manatees all day.

Any pet peeves? Mostly just white people who say "for shizzle."

What historical figure would you most like to meet and why? Joan of Arc. Because she was seventeen, a rebel, and she didn't give a rat's ass what people thought. Basically, my hero.

I have not yet agreed to do the show—only promised that I would sit, listen, and do this dog and pony meeting so that if I chose not to do the show, I would at least not absorb the guilt of not considering it when my family was facing total homelessness. Doc told me the THE NETWORK execs only want to meet me without the rest of my family around. That explains why I find myself sitting across a table from two stylishly dressed women and an Izod sweater–wearing guy telling them the horrifying trauma that was learning the origin of my name.

"And how did that make you feel when your mom told you how she came to name you Emery?" asks the younger of the two ladies. The chick is stick-thin, with dark hair cut harshly with bangs, and wearing those polyester-looking kind of pants that are so unsexy you have to call them "slacks." Her hair is pulled back in a bun so tightly I wonder if it's the cause of the perma-grimace on her face.

"It made me feel nothing, really," I reply. "I mean, I don't know if I felt anything. Like, maybe I *thought* something. But feel? No."

"Then what did you think?" she pressed.

"I guess it made me think I was useful," I say. "Emery boards, you know, at least have a purpose. They actually do something. I mean, think about it. Angels aren't even real."

The three execs get a good chuckle out of that zinger. Meanwhile, all I can think is that it's three o'clock and I haven't eaten since noon, back in the dark ages when I scarfed down a couple of double-cheese quesadillas with sour cream and extra-hot salsa topped off with a contraband Twix bar I had stashed in my panties drawer, before Mom drove me an hour up the 405 to this Palace of Pop Culture.

This meeting has to end ASAP. Seriously.

The older boss-lady, sitting cross-legged in her tight black skirt, scribbles notes in the yellow legal pad resting on her lap. The buzz-cut hipster guy rubs his goatee and nods like a knowing professor at everything I say. As I talk, they scan my body as if I am a zoo specimen, while Doc sits at the table on my right, his yellowing Chiclet teeth gleaming with ego and pride and annoying Britishness, fearing I will screw up and say the wrong thing at any point. A valid concern.

"Tell us more about your family," the dude exec says, leaning forward. "Let's start with your sister."

"What do you want to know?"

"Do you get along?"

"Not really. We are sisters, biologically. Everything else about us is different. She likes sports; I hate them. She is a size two; I am not. She is obsessed with being pretty; I clearly am not." Doc starts scratching his head. He doesn't like where this is going, not that I can blame him. "Angel is kind of a bitch, to be totally honest. She doesn't care about anyone but herself and is obsessed with her looks. That's why I feel bad for her. But I suppose not everyone can be perfect—like me."

The room is silent, as if they're all shocked that this obese teenager with major attitude is so delusional she thinks she's *perfect*.

"I'm just kidding, guys!" I say before they get too misled. "As you can tell from my grubby appearance and my inability to be polite, I am far from perfect."

"Emery isn't afraid to speak her mind," Doc butts in.

The older boss lady has sandy blonde hair, is as fit as a workout model and good-looking enough to be a movie star. She reminds me of Jennifer Aniston, but with a few more lines around her eyes and on her forehead. She also hasn't said a word yet—and her silence is creeping me out. In fact, it's about as unsettling as the hurricane that's starting to brew in my stomach. Shouldn't have had that salsa. *Really* shouldn't have had that salsa.

"Are you close to your dad?" the dark-haired lady, herself quite plump, asks.

"Physically, yes. Because we do live in the same house. Emotionally, not so much."

"Why's that?" she asks with empathetic eyes. "Why aren't you closer?"

"Um, probably because he's out of town all the time. And because he puts most of his energy and focus on 'The One and Only.'"

"The One and Only?" she asks.

"Angel," I say. "You know, God's grand gift to mankind. The Chosen One."

The hipster exec folds his hands in prayer and observes caringly, "That must be painful to be constantly compared to your sister."

"It's fine," I say without emotion. "Dad and I don't like the same things anyway. Basketball, baseball, soccer, anything athletic—I hate them all. And yeah, I tend to like foods that are not necessarily the healthiest. I am not a health nut like the rest of my family. The only part that bugs me is that I think he's embarrassed by me. I feel like the only thing we have in common is some DNA. I call myself the fat sheep of the family."

The three corporate stooges scribble a little more into their notepads. As they bury their heads in their notes, I take the opportunity to secretly slide my hand down to stretch out the elastic waistband of my underwear. Damn thing is digging into my gut, which is bloated with a giant gas bubble. I wiggle in my chair, trying to encourage the air to pass down through my body oh-so quietly.

"So, Emery." The dark-haired exec uncrosses her legs and crosses them again. "Do you have any favorite shows? Do you even watch any reality TV?"

"I don't watch most of them," I say. "There are just some shows that I couldn't bring myself to watch, like that show about nuns who work as loggers near the Bering Strait." I scratch my scalp. "Come to think of it, I'd rather watch real people's YouTube videos than most reality TV shows."

"Do you think you could open up your life like most reality stars do? It can be very invasive. Unscripted television is not for everybody. That's a big reason why we wanted to meet with you today. Doc has told us *a lot* about you and your family. We've met everyone else, as you know. Now we really just want to get to know you better."

The hipster guy is wearing a pair of thick black-frame glasses that make him look smarter than he probably is. He glances down at my questionnaire. "I see here that you list Jenna Marbles as a 'hero' of yours. Who is this Jenna Marbles person?"

He doesn't know who Jenna Marbles is? He doesn't know that she is the coolest, most honest, hugest female vlogger in the history of YouTube and has over five million subscribers? Mr. Hipster Guy must not know that Jenna, who is in her twenties but speaks so brutally honestly that she is relatable to all females, makes videos in which she rants about things like how horrendously self-loathing it is that girls hate on each other so much, points out how stupid guys are, harshes on how vacuous girls can be chatting on the Web, riffs on the overall absurdity of the male obsession with Internet porn, and does a spot-on impersonation of Ke$ha.

In other words, Mr. Hipster Guy is not very hip at all. He is proof that you can dress like a hipster, you can wear glasses like a hipster, and you can grow a goatee like a hipster. But all these things make you actually hip as much as Spanx makes you actually thin.

But rather than be the arrogant, judgmental, precocious teenager that my mom has been trying to make me not be, I opt to pretend that I am not at all disgusted by this "creative exec" not knowing that Jenna Marbles is my generation's Helen Gurley Brown.[6]

"Oh, Jenna is just so real," I say. "I love her. Google her."

They stare at me. No one is talking. "I'm an open book," I exclaim to break the awkwardness.

"I see that." She laughs. "So do you think you would be up for doing a show, especially one about you trying to lose weight?"

"Honestly?" I ask.

The lady looks at her two colleagues and glances back at me. "Yes, we want honesty. Reality television requires honesty perhaps more than any other quality."

I want to say "not to mention profoundly pathological narcissism"—but I bite my tongue. The stated purpose of this

---

[6] Helen Gurley Brown, the editor-in-chief of *Cosmo* magazine, and the first real feminist to speak to women on a candid level. Last year in Social I read about her book *Sex and the Single Girl*, which came out in the 1960s but is still amazing. If she were alive, she'd be doing what Jenna Marbles is doing and be a YouTube superstar.

meeting, at least as Doc coached me beforehand, is to win these network tools over.

"Yes, I do think I can let it all hang out," I say. "Why the hell not?" Doc smiles. He clearly likes this line. "If I were any more honest I would be running the Girl Scouts."

That line finally elicits a sound from the heretofore silent Blonde Ice Queen in Heels.

"So I take it you don't watch THE NETWORK?" the boss says.

"Not really," I reply.

"Why's that?"

"Because it's boring. Super boring. No offense, but all your shows are way too touchy-feel-good for me. Teens giving moms makeovers. Sick kids meeting their favorite celebrity before they die. Then there's that show about celebrity good deeds. It's all a little too dork-a-licious for my tastes, sorry to say. No offense. I mean, if they are so-called reality shows, shouldn't they at least be capturing reality? They all look so staged and phony and just about as fake as my sister's breasts."

If Doc's shoulders grew any stiffer, I'd suspect they were under the influence of Viagra. In a few venomous sentences, I had managed to disparage his entire body of work. Understandably, he has that shut-up-while-you're-ahead look on his face when he stands up and adds, "What Emery is trying to say is that maybe THE NETWORK is not her demographic."

The older lady takes off her glasses in that way that people do when they want to look like they're getting serious.

"Actually," she says, "Emery is right. Most of our reality programming *is* boring. It tends to be sappy and predictable and manipulative and just not very entertaining. That's why our ratings were down thirty percent this year. That's why we need a hit. Emery, this network needs more genuine characters like you." She points her silver ballpoint pen in my direction, and I look back over my shoulder, just in case someone is quietly lurking behind me. But no one is, and I realize the woman, who is the president of THE NETWORK, is talking about little ol' me.

"You, my dear, aren't afraid to speak your mind. We have been trying to convince viewers that all our shows are honest and real and genuine, but they're not. They are formula and for-matted. They have lost their spark, and our ratings are suffering because of it. Why? Because our core viewer is someone like you: smart, young, bold, sassy, and ready to entertain and be entertained. And you just identified another major flaw in our programming scheme with your answer about Jennifer Marballs."

"Jenna Marbles," I correct her.

"Yes, her," she continues. "We want to attract viewers fifteen to twenty-five years old, but we aren't putting enough content on the platform they want or from the point of view they want."

I am starting to feel better about basically telling them they all suck at their jobs. Yet my stomach is not feeling better. In fact, all I really want to do is excuse myself and take care of some business in private.

Before I can do so, Boss Lady interjects, "The real question is, do you think you can lose the weight? Can you lose fifty pounds in fifty days? This will require a major effort and dedica-tion on your part."

"Fifty pounds?" I shoot evil-eye darts at Doc. "No one told me anything about fifty pounds in fifty days. Is that what you want me to do?"

"Yes," says the Boss Lady. "That is, at the core, what the show is about. And how your family is going to help you get there. Are you up for this challenge?"

I clench my teeth and look straight at my reflection in the shiny wood top of the conference table. I focus my eyes so hard crinkles form around my eyes. And then nature—well, nature happens. A bubble of air releases itself from the prison that is my body. It's loud. A very loud, conspicuous, and rude air bubble. Okay, it is a fart.

Reflexively my rear end pops up like an inch above my chair, and I let out a cough to mask the sound of the gaseous release. But it's too late. The entire room obviously knows I have just cut some major cheese.

Five seconds later, I still have not looked up. I still stare at the tabletop. I'm so consumed with the fear that the gas is going to stink up this tiny conference room that I can't even remember what the Boss Lady has just asked me.

"What was the question?"

"It's okay," the Boss Lady says, closing her spiral notebook as the other two excuse themselves and run for fresher air outside the room. "I think we've heard enough. We will be in touch."

Later that night, Mom gets a phone call from Doc. She scampers out to the back porch and returns a few minutes later with a smile as wide as Nevada.

"Girls, I've got some good news! Doc says THE NETWORK wants to do a show with us! They're sending over contracts tomorrow!"

I'm lounging on my favorite corner spot on the living room couch playing Angry Birds. Angel, who has been doing yoga on the floor beside me, jumps up and down with Mom like they are giddy pageant queens.

"Let's call Daddy!" Angel says, skipping away to grab her phone upstairs.

Mom plops down onto the couch next to me. She's so light the cushion barely sinks.

"Does Angel know about the house situation?" I ask her.

"No. No one is supposed to know, including you until you snooped. Daddy doesn't want Angel to be worried."

"And I take it Doc knows."

"Yes, I had to tell him," she says.

"So Doc knows that you're desperate. Great move. Not."

Mom lifts her feet onto the couch and hugs her knees. "I'm just trying to save this family," she says. "I want you to get healthy; I want Angel to get famous; I want Dad to not be so stressed. You have to understand I am doing what is in the best interests of all of us."

"Does Dad know that I know we are going to be homeless and bankrupt unless I do this show?"

"No," she exhales. "I haven't told him you found out. Before he left for his convention this week in Phoenix, he told me he didn't want you to know about the money troubles. He doesn't want you to do the show for the wrong reason. He wants you to do the show so that you can have freedom."

THURSDAY, NOVEMBER 14

"Lana Sinclair has never done anything like this before," Mom enthuses. "This is a *really* big deal. Really big."

I am unimpressed. "Who's Lana Sinclair?"

"Oh, just the most powerful woman in television is all," Mom says. "She's the older woman you met with yesterday at THE NETWORK. The gorgeous blonde. She runs THE NETWORK. She used to be a model. In fact, she and I used to compete against each other in pageants growing up, back in grade school. She's really made a name for herself since then."

"Oh, you're talking about the Boss Lady. She's heading over here now? To our house?"

"Yes, she and Doc are coming with a contract for us to sign." She does an up-and-down on me. "So . . ." Mom gives me her infamous Judgmental Once-Over. "Is this what you're wearing?"

I have on my favorite black men's XL-size Van Halen T-shirt and purple cotton sweatpants. I'm a slave to comfort, not fashion. So I ignore her condescending question, which is rhetorical anyway.

Mom goes back to nervously rushing around the house with a rag, wiping surfaces that don't need wiping. I guess this makes her feel in control. Mom cleans; I eat. And Angel coats her face in makeup and starves herself. I suppose that we all have our vices. Mine just happens to be the most fun.

Angel, meanwhile, has assumed her usual position: standing in front of the mirror in our bathroom, applying more makeup than a drag queen.

Ding, dong.

Mom rushes to the front door and lets in Doc and Lana Sinclair. Lana looks even more stunningly beautiful than she did yesterday at the meeting. She's wearing three-inch heels, a beige skirt to just above her knees, and a classy black silk blouse. Her blonde hair is pulled back in a ponytail. She's around the same age as Mom, but looks younger, probably because she does more Botox and has had more work done. Doc is wearing his typical uniform of brown, shiny loafers, blue jeans, and a button-down shirt unbuttoned at the top so that his horrid chest hairs sprout out.

"Sorry about my gas issues yesterday," I apologize to Lana. "Mexican food. Lesson learned."

"No worries," Lana says. "We've all been there."

Mom walks them to the living room and offers them a cup of tea, which they politely decline as Angel dramatically walks in wearing a tight, white jean skirt and even tighter top. Doc leers at her. If I automatically lost a pound for every time I've seen Doc inappropriately check out my sister, I would be one very skinny bitch. In fact, we would be able to skip this entire reality fiasco altogether.

Mom, Angel, and I sit in the armchairs on the opposite side of the couch.

"Where's Jasper?" Doc asks.

"Bettendorf, Iowa," Mom replies. "He's speaking at the Change Your Life convention there. Then he's off to Buffalo for another speech."

"I assume he's still on board," Doc says. "He realizes he is expected to appear on camera now and then, right? Especially for the live shows. This is very important."

"More than ever," Mom assures him. "He said he will FedEx a signed contract tonight. Jasper is a man of his word."

"Okay, good, jolly good." Doc reaches into his tattered leather mail carrier bag, places the contract in front of us on the glass coffee table, and defers to Lana.

"Ladies, this is the contract for all of you to star in a reality series for our network that we would like to call *Fifty Pounds to Freedom*," Lana says with purpose. "The show would be about Emery's bold, inspiring effort to lose fifty pounds in fifty days with the help and support of you, her loving family, not to mention a team of the world's top experts in diet, fitness, and mental health care. Imagine the weight-loss challenge of *The Biggest Loser* but with a greater challenge. With the family docu-dynamics of the Kardashians but, of course, with a much more relatable family. With the intimacy of *Big Brother*—but with a purpose. You know what that makes?"

Lana silenced me when she called my family relatable.

"Groundbreaking television is what!" she answers.

Mom and Angel, eyes popped wide open with blank stares, nod and smile stiffly in agreement. Lana is impressive. She is eloquent, pretty, and earnest. But I can see through it all and realize she's just another TV exec looking for ratings and to get her executive bonus.

"And Emery," Lana faces me, "you will be happy to know that *Fifty Pounds to Freedom* will also take a few pointers from your Web girl Jenna Marbles."

Lana pulls out an iPad from her oversize designer bag and flips it open in front of me. "This will be our first reality show to feature a 24-7 YouTube channel dedicated to your own commentary. That means that you can be your own Jenna Marbles and post videos whenever you want."

I look at the screen and see a NETWORK-branded page featuring a picture of me underneath a giant headline FIFTY POUNDS TO FREEDOM.

"I can post whatever video I want?" I ask. "Like Jenna Marbles does?"

"Basically yes, as long as the content is not offensive and meets our network standards," Lana says. "What you said in yesterday's meeting was right on point, and I already have our Digital Team at THE NETWORK setting up YouTube pages for all of our other THE NETWORK talent. This kind of content, this raw footage, is vital and will complement the fine documentary-style work being shot by Doc and his team."

She points and adds, "We've already designed what the site will look like. Fans can follow your journey whenever they want on your channel, and then every Sunday night, they'll tune in for the live weigh-in show."

"Weigh-in show?" I ask.

"Well, yeah," Doc explains. "The show will air every

Wednesday and Sunday at nine o'clock. But at the end of every Sunday's show we will end with a live weigh-in, in which you simply stand on a scale and get weighed."

Scales scare me. So of all the things just told to me, this comment is the one that causes my stomach to cramp.

"We think this kind of dramatic reveal each week will make for positively riveting television," Lana adds. "And for every pound you lose, we will pay you a thousand dollars."

She closes the iPad. "If you lose the entire fifty pounds in fifty days, your family gets the prize. Simple as that."

Doc adds with a devilish grin, "That means: One. Million. Dollars."

His British accent only adding to his already existing tendency to pump up the Shakespearean-esque dramatics, Doc holds up a silver Montblanc ballpoint pen. "All you have to do is sign and your lives will change for the better."

"And what if I don't lose the weight?" I ask.

Doc and Lana look at each other, then back at me. "We're not going to worry about that, Emery," Lana says. "We believe in you. We are rooting for you. You can do it."

Angel grabs the pen and instantly signs on the black line on the last page of the contract. She places the pen down and patty-cake claps like a toddler. "Yay!" she exclaims.

Mom takes her pen and asks, "When would this start?"

"We're looking at Monday, December second, but with a series premiere show the night before to set up what is about to happen," Lana says. "Our audience research shows that there will be very little competition on other networks in this period, especially around the holidays. And the holidays, of course, is a time for families to be together. This being more than anything a show about the power of family to come together to achieve a common goal, we think we have a winning formula here."

"That's in just over two weeks," Mom points out. "Isn't that kind of soon?"

"I have the best production crew in the business," Doc says. "I have taken the best shooters and field producers available. I have assembled an all-star team. Nothing but the best for you and your family, Brandi."

Mom grins. She glances at me and our eyes lock, though I show no emotion as she looks away and signs her name. She places the pen down.

"Boom," she says, high-fiving Angel.

Doc hands me the pen. "It's all you, Emery."

Unlike Angel and Mom, I pick up the thirty-page contract and start scanning it. At the very top of the first page, **<u>IN BOLD CAPS AND UNDERLINE FONT</u>**, is a warning: "**<u>DO NOT SIGN THIS UNTIL YOU HAVE READ IT COMPLETELY</u>**." I pretend I don't have four sets of eyeballs laser-beaming on me and actually glance at it.

I'm no lawyer, and I read about every third line, but from what I can read, "THE NETWORK and Producers" are basically not responsible for anything whatsoever that could go wrong and by signing I acknowledge such things like . . .

- My participation could result in death, loss of limbs, and mental illness such as "nervous breakdowns."
- Should I undergo any medical procedures while involved in the show, I risk not-so-awesome things like infection, disfigurement, and (again) death.
- I agree to be possibly humiliated and explicitly portrayed "in a false light."

- I may be filmed naked or "partially nude" at any time.

- If I contract AIDS or other sexually transmitted diseases ["gonorrhea, herpes, syphilis, pelvic inflammatory disease (PID), chlamydia, scabies (crabs), hepatitis, genital warts, and other communicable and sexually transmitted diseases, or pregnancy, etc."] while filming, THE NETWORK is not responsible.

- I agree not to get pregnant, and if I do, they can terminate the agreement immediately.

- I grant the Producer and Network rights to my life story either in book, TV, movie, or any digital form, and as such, they can alter my life story, including misrepresenting it as 100 percent fiction.

- I agree to wear a two-piece bikini, the style of which will be consulted with and approved by Producers, for each live weigh-in show.

- I promise not to hide from cameras in establishments where they can't film and agree that they can film me with hidden cameras and any footage shot prior to signing this agreement can be used in Production.

- I authorize the Producer to have total access to my school records, government forms, bank account information, etc., including any computers or phones used during the course of filming Production.

- The production can show up at my house at any time to film and/or take any thing they want, as long as they return the objects once production has ended.

- For one year after the show's final episode airs, we are required to participate in all producer-determined press and forbidden from engaging in any media (radio, television, chat rooms, blogs) without THE NETWORK/Producers' express written permission.

- They own the copyright to every photograph, email, website, sound or video recording, and documented performance created in relation to the Program, in every medium imaginable.

- The explicit list of physical challenges I might be subjected to include traveling by "air (whether via helicopter, commercial airliner, glider, private aircraft, or otherwise), train and/or automobile, as well as strenuous and/or dangerous and/or mental activity—including but not limited to, horseback riding, jogging, bicycling, motorcycling, exercise and/or weight equipment, skydiving, swimming, bungee jumping, parasailing, snorkeling, jet skiing, amusement park activities, rock climbing, engaging in contact sports, hiking, kayaking, and boating."

After spending a good two minutes reading over the legalese, and I don't even get halfway through it, I put it down on the coffee table, stand up, and tell Doc, "You're kidding, right?"

"Kidding about what?" he says.

"That I would be dumb-ass enough to sign this."

"It's a standard contract. And please don't curse."

Doc picks up the sheaf of paper that is heavy enough that, if dropped on a poodle, would cause major injury. "There is nothing in here that any reality show star in history has not already signed a thousand times."

"Honey, can I have a word with you?" Mom says, curling her forefinger in my face like a wicked witch. "In the kitchen. Now."

Before leaving the room, Mom turns to Doc and Lana. "Give us a moment." Angel quietly follows.

I assume my usual "Team Meeting" position on the dark wood stool at the counter next to Angel. It's hard to be in the kitchen and not have a craving for those peanut butter cookies that Mom hid behind the crackers on the second shelf from the top in the pantry. But I am able to restrain myself. For now.

"Emery, what is your attitude all of a sudden?" Mom says. "If everyone read every single line of every agreement in life, no one would ever do anything. Sometimes you just have to take a leap of faith."

"A leap off a cliff," I crack. "You have always told all of us we should never sign anything without reading it first or giving it to a lawyer to look at. But all of a sudden, you just want me to go and sign away—"

"We can't afford a lawyer," she interrupts. "Dad's business is suffering a little cash-flow problem at the moment."

"You're being so selfish!" Angel whines before I can even respond to Mom's economic revelation. "Have you thought about me? Have you realized that this could launch my TV hosting career? I could waste four years of my life going to college for broadcast journalism, then beg stations to give me an internship, and then beg some more for them to put me on the air. Or I can be on this huge reality show and, like, be instantly famous."

Fearing I am about to foil their fame-whoring plot, Mom is pacing in that frantic way she does whenever she feels like she has lost control of a situation. That's when she reaches up into the cupboard above the toaster and does what she usually does when she *really* has lost control of a situation. She pulls down a pill bottle and adds, "This is *such* a big deal. To all of us."

She twists open the white plastic top and drops two tiny white pills into her palm. She swallows each individually and chases them with a swig of water.

"Look, Em," she continues. "What else can I do here? You know how badly we want this. How much we need this money. This will make Angel's hosting career. Also, don't forget that your father is in the motivational speaking business. Just think what this could do for him. And hello, you will get healthy. We are all on board. What else can I do or say to convince you?"

"Well, there is something," I say.

"What?"

"The million bucks we get if I lose the weight. Who gets all that money?"

"Our family, of course," she replies. "It will go into our family account probably."

"Nope," I say. "That's not where it's going."

"Then where do you propose it goes?"

"Half to the family, half to me. It's only fair."

I stand up and pull Angel's chair back as she's sitting in it. "Time to go, Angel. I need a private moment with Mom."

She huffs and looks at Mom. "It's okay, honey. Just go and sit with Lana and Doc. Tell them we are coming in a minute." Angel stands, straightens her skirt, and wiggles her little rear out of the room.

"You know that I saw the foreclosure letter. The total owed is $498,000. So even though I suck at my math, I believe that means that a half a million bucks should cover that bill. You don't need any more. I do. And since you can't do it without me . . ."

Mom paces the floor with her hands on her hips. She stops and faces me. "So what you're saying is that if you get half, then you will sign the contract?"

"Yes." I extend my right hand toward her and open my palm. "Shake?" If my mom is going to put the proverbial gun to my head, I think it's only fair I put it to hers.

Mom drops her hands to her side. "Hold on here. What exactly do you plan on doing with the money?"

"Buy myself true freedom," I reply. "Because, contrary to whatever you guys think, I won't be finding freedom on your moronic, exploitive, train wreck of a reality show."

Of course, Mom agrees to my offer and we shake on it.

Of course, she agrees to let me be home-schooled while the show is being filmed, which is awesome since that means I won't have to see the Highland Beach Mean Girls.

Of course, Angel bounces up and down and assures Lana

and Doc she will do the best job possible and then immediately makes a waxing appointment.

Of course, Doc practically pops a boner when I sign away my life.

Of course, I celebrate by eating all fourteen peanut butter cookies left in the package in the pantry.

II. SOUP OR SALAD

MONDAY, NOVEMBER 18

After third-period English, I make my way past a row of lockers and step into the courtyard, where the usual cliques have clustered with about as much crossover as the Israelis and Palestinians.

Josh and the other football and volleyball jocks stand next to the soda machine. I avoid making eye contact and slink around the long way, avoiding them all together. I don't need more Josh drama.

As for the Drama Nerds, they are harmless, and are clustered harmlessly around the middle picnic table. In the middle of everyone, yet not quite belonging to anyone. There's something noble about that.

The Brats, meanwhile, hover on the other side of the soda machine, just close enough to soak in the aura of the jocks, but separate enough to play hard to get. Naturally, this isn't where I belong, which is why I brazenly step up to cheer captain Kendra, the unofficial leader of The Brats.

Our freshman year, the Highland High yearbook dubbed her "Kool Kendra," instantly vaulting her to "It" status, meaning Angel just *had* to become BFFs with her, a goal she wrote down on a piece of paper taped to her bathroom mirror and ultimately achieved. The two frenemies are going on two years now. Kendra would never give me the time of day if I weren't Angel's sister, but since I am, she has to at least acknowledge my existence.

Kendra is standing with the usual gaggle of towering volleyball girls, fellow cheer sluts, and associated band of makeup-coated bro hos as she texts on her phone. Her long brown hair flows down onto her shoulders with the perfection of a pageant queen. All this makes me want to annoy her. And since I have no self-control, this is exactly what I set out to do.

"What's up, Kendra?" I ask.

"I don't know," she replies with a sneer. "What?"

"That's why I'm asking you, because I want to know what's up."

"Be more specific." Kendra doesn't look up from her phone. She's probably sexting a college boy. "I'm busy."

"Douchebagsezwhat?" I mumble.

"What?" Kendra takes her eyes off her phone. "What?"

"Douchebagsezwhat." This time I say it even faster and even less understandable.

"What?" Now she's really confused. "Your sister is right. You are seriously retarded, Emery."

"Oh, forget it." I smile brightly. "Sorry to bother you."

"What are you talking about? Seriously, Emery." Kendra puts her hand on her chin and strokes it. "Oh, I mean, seriously, dear Emery. I know all about you."

Even though covered in layers of fat, I can feel my stomach knot. "What do you mean?"

"Oh," Kendra says. "I think you know exactly what I'm talking about." She walks away and stops on her heels. She throws me a smug look. "I know your secret."

I narrow my eyes and stare her down as Kendra steps closer and puts her hand on my shoulder. "But it's okay; your dirty little secret is safe with me," she says. "I got your back."

Her gaggle then waddles into our conversation and I pretend nothing out of the ordinary just happened.

"So," I change topic, "did Angel tell you the news? About our show?"

"Yes, she did," Kendra says. "Maje congrats." She drapes her arm fully around me and makes a puppy-dog face. "And you know, Emery, I really hope this show helps you not be so fat and angry. And *easy*."

THURSDAY, NOVEMBER 21

My Thanksgiving Dinner Menu:

Seven fat slices of turkey = 550 calories

Three scoops of stuffing = 470 calories

Three scoops of mashed potatoes with butter = 545 calories

Three dinner rolls = 228 calories

Macaroni and cheese = 207 calories

Turkey gravy = 140 calories

Cranberry sauce = 172 calories

Two slices of pumpkin pie = 632 calories

One slice of pecan pie = 503 calories

Total calories = 3,447

Value of Knowing This Caloric Goodness Is Equivalent to
My Last Supper = Pricele$$

SUNDAY, DECEMBER 1

Patriotic music. Drums and flutes and violins.

"Welcome to a new kind of reality show. A show about controlling our own destiny."

An American flag ripples in the wind atop the White House. Children sit on blankets eating at a picnic.

"A show about being free."

Shots of pickup trucks and kids playing baseball and swimming in the ocean.

"A show as American as apple pie."

An aerial shot above Highland Beach, pushing in from the waves and down the beachside homes.

"Welcome to the world of sixteen-year-old American Emery Jackson—and her family. What you're about to see is the most *real* reality show you've ever seen. This is *Fifty Pounds to Freedom*!"

It shouldn't surprise me that Doc has opted to be "the voice" of the show and do all the hyperdramatic voice-overs, but I am a little. I mean, you'd think making millions off exploiting desperate wannabe reality stars would be enough to inflate his ego balloon.

"Over the next fifty days, starting at midnight tonight, until January 20, you will witness this courageous teenager's battle with the bulge. She will be inspired and pushed to the limits by a team of trainers, nutrition experts, mental health experts, as well as a few surprise mentors to help her along the way. You will see her transform her life of shame and constraint into one of happiness and freedom. Every Sunday night you will see her journey from the previous week, and at the end of each episode, she will take to the Freedom Meals® scale LIVE . . . and weigh in."

We're watching the premiere at Lucky Lulu's pub down by the beach and Mom has invited all our friends. The crowd erupts in applause when it goes to commercial (an ad for the BlAsstMaster 2000® exercise ball—only $49.99! . . . plus shipping and handling).[7] The two cameramen that constantly surround us now also have come along, shooting everything we do, and say—documenting every fart, urinary, gastrointestinal, and bowel movement and every single food-like product I ingest. We all wear mics clipped to our shirts, connected to wire leading to battery packs that are hooked onto the back of our pants. This will be our wired reality for the next fifty days.

"Meet Emery Jackson. She's a junior at Highland High in sunny Highland Beach, California. But Emery's teenage life is not so sunny. Like eighteen percent of teens in America, she is clinically obese. This weight problem of our youth is nothing short of an epidemic. Junk food, video games, and hand-held electronic devices have only worsened matters for our teens.

---

[7] Which is another $14.99, which brings the cost of this cheap rubber ball that will eventually end up dusty and deflated in your garage to $64.98.

And the face of that epidemic is Emery Jackson."

The first episode has been entirely taped, shot over the last week, and starts with an introduction to me and our family and my weight-loss goal, all in Doc's British accent, which he is over-doing to the point that he sounds like Richard Branson.

Suddenly they start showing me in a series of pathetic situations. Playing beach volleyball like a beached whale. Binge eating waffles late at night in the kitchen. Scarfing down Thanksgiving dinner last week. Shaking my naked jelly belly while standing in the mirror counting, "One Mississippi, Two Mississippi . . ." And I realize that all this footage was shot without me knowing. Hidden cameras must have been documenting me for weeks!

I stomp in the direction of Mom. "What the hell is this?" I demand.

"What?" She keeps her focus on the big-screen TV above the bar. "Isn't this amazing?"

"You guys didn't tell me I was on a hidden freakin' camera the entire time." I tug on her arm. "That is so not okay."

"Emery, dear," she says quietly. "This is what we signed up for. We just have to learn to deal with it. It will all be worth it. Trust me."

I glare, knowing she is right. I am the fool who signed up for this. Mom goes back to staring at herself on TV, as if this is the biggest moment of her life. It is the lowest of mine, and I storm out of the bar.

I head for the sand and as I am about to reach the foot of the pier, I look back and see Ben running after me, and a cameraman running behind him. They catch up to me as I'm slogging toward a dune near the shore.

"Emery, what's wrong?" Ben asks, settling down onto the sand beside me.

"I think I've made a big mistake. I can't do this. All this attention. All this expectation. Pressure. I feel like I'm not going to be able to lose the weight and I will be a total embarrassment."

Ben puts his arm around me, and we watch the waves.

"You're going to be great, Em. You are the strongest person I know. You've just never flexed these kinds of muscles before."

"That's funny." I make a bicep curl and point at the formless blob that is supposed to be a muscle. "What muscles?"

"The weight-loss ones, Em. Just because it is a new thing doesn't mean you can't do it. You can do it."

I want to tell Ben that what upset me more than discovering they had used hidden camera footage on the show was seeing myself on TV for the first time and realizing just how huge of a beast I have become. I've always heard a TV camera adds ten pounds, but in my case, it looks more like 100 pounds and it is the most depressing thing I have ever seen. In that moment of seeing my giant body, I saw things I had never noticed before:

- My thighs are so wide that they run together when I walk, making me waddle.

- My face is rounder than a cherry tomato.

- My arms are a formless mass of fatty tissue that jiggles when I move even in the slightest.

- My chin is all but gone, and has been replaced by three distinct rolls of fat that are forming butt-like cracks around my throat.

- My torso is so round and thick that I look like I swallowed a doggie bed and it jammed sideways into my stomach.

As I consider telling Ben all these crushing observations I'm making of my pathetic self, I realize there is a camera zooming in on us from about thirty yards away. And that I'm wearing a mic. When we started with the mics earlier this week I thought I would never be able to forget I was wearing them and being filmed.

Ben pulls me in tighter, and we sit in silence and listen to the waves crash.

"I have something for you," Ben says, pulling out a box from the front pocket of his jacket. "Go ahead, open it."

"I didn't realize I was on *The Bachelor*," I joke.

"Just open the damn thing." He grins.

I lift off the top of the tiny box and inside lies a necklace. It is silver, my favorite. When I lift it out of the box, a manatee figure the size of a quarter dangles from the bottom.

"You like?" he asks sheepishly.

"Me definitely likey." I hug him. "It's so adorable! And so are you."

Ben has to be the most genuine, sincere, and vulnerable soul ever to walk the streets of Highland, which, granted, may not be offering him much competition.

"So, good," he says. "But I just want you to know that no matter how big or small you are, no matter how hard this journey will be for you, that I will always think of you as my perfect little manatee."

"Fat and happy?"

"No. Just happy."

I put on the necklace, and I feel tears well up. Just as I'm about to let the tear drop from the bottom of my eye onto my cheek, a hand drapes over my shoulder. And it's not Ben's. No, this hand is way too hairy and wrinkly. And its stubby fingers are creepier than a '70s porn star 'stache.

"Kids, kids, kids," Doc says, patting my shoulder. "That was amazing. Great stuff. But can we do it again? We need to shoot the reverse angle."

"So much for reality," I crack. "Are you F-ing kidding me?"

"No," Doc answers harshly, ripping the headphones from his ears. "This is a show and this is how a show is produced, darling. The biggest reality stars in the business always shoot a scene more than once. You remember when Alberto proposed to Annie on Season Six? They shot that fourteen times. And yes, it was dramatic and memorable. You know what take they used? Number thirteen. They would have used the last take but the audio was dirty. I heard it was a leaf blower in the background. In any event, let's just do a retake. With the same emotion."

Doc puts his headphones back on, presumably so he can hear our audio, as the cameraman repositions about twenty yards in front of me and Ben.

"Is that guy on crack?" Ben asks.

"Crack is whack," I joke.

"Action!" Doc shouts from down at the bottom of the dune.

Ben and I look at each other and burst out in laughter. And suddenly we are actors.

After faking our way through the reenactment, Doc announces that the inaugural live weigh-in is in less than an hour and orders Ryan, the sandy-blond surfer-boy PA who serves as Doc's personal gofer, to give us a ride back to my house, where each weigh-in will take place.

"That was really special," Ryan says as he drives us the mile back home in the SUV. "It was so real. We usually don't see that kind of reality in any of these shows." He twists his neck and looks back at us. "Please don't tell Doc I said that."

"No worries." I laugh. "I try to talk to Doc as little as possible anyway."

"You sure you can do this tonight?" Ben asks as we pull into the driveway. "You know, the bikini thing for the weigh-in."

"I guess we'll see, huh?"

"I don't get it," Ben replies.

"Get what?"

"How you overnight have gone from being the last girl I would ever expect to wear a bikini to someone who is actually willing to wear one and do so on national television."

"Ben, we all spend so much of our lives hiding things," I say, acutely aware of the camera mounted on the rearview mirror recording my speech. "We hide secrets from the people we love. We hide food in underwear drawers. We hide our bodies underneath clothes. What this show is making me realize is that I don't want to be a hider anymore. I want to be a show-er. And if that means wearing a bikini, I am going to do it. At this point, there is no shame to my game."

Back home, Ben joins Angel, Mom, and Dad in the living room, which the crew has theatrically lit like a Broadway stage. Flashy blues and reds stripe the back wall, as the giant digital scale is illuminated by a spotlight. The oversize screen reading **0.00 LBS** rests on a stand next to the scale, just waiting to be increased exponentially with my human load.

The cameraman and cute PA Ryan follow me into my bedroom, where I find two sets of bikinis set out on my bed. Also laid out is a white terry-cloth bathrobe with FIFTY POUNDS TO FREEDOM stitched onto the back in pink lettering. One of the swimsuits is black, the other white. Both, thank God, are not the string bikini kind with the dental-floss butt patch. In fact, the bottoms are "swim short" style.

I kick out Ryan and the camera guy and enter the bathroom, the one place I have discovered there aren't any cameras—even hidden ones.

Because black is a "slimming" color, I slide into that one. And by "slide" I mean wiggle frantically in the strained manner in which a magician extricates himself from a straitjacket.

Knock, knock, knock.

I put on the robe and open the door to find Doc standing there in a tuxedo and wearing more makeup than a Highland Beach housewife.

"Are you ready to do this, superstar?" he asks.

THE NETWORK really must think I am going to lose the weight and have to pay me a million bones, because they must already be cutting costs by hiring a ragged-looking Brit to host this. So much for THE NETWORK wanting to appeal to young females.

"I'm as ready as I will ever be," I say.

"Splendid," Doc says. "We go live in five minutes. Let's commence." He turns to lead me down to the living room but then stops himself. "One last thing, my darling. I was really hoping you'd go with white. It will make you look, um, larger. It will be more dramatic."

"And if I don't?"

"Oh." A devilish smile curls upward from his cracked, sunburnt lips. "You will."

I stay back, and though I hate myself for doing it, change into the white bikini.

Downstairs, more people are packed into the living room than attended our Halloween party. There are sound guys, lighting guys, a stage director, a teleprompter operator, three cameramen, a makeup artist, two security guards, a couple of producers, and standing alone in the back is THE NETWORK's Lana Sinclair. Our eyes link as I stand beside the scale. She smiles and nods approvingly.

"Ten seconds!" announces the stage director. "Quiet everyone. Nine, eight . . ."

As he counts, I notice Angel has her arms crossed in front of her with a disgusted look on her face. Then I immediately realize what's wrong. I am the center of attention, not her. And it must be tearing her up inside. If I were a more enlightened, compassionate person, maybe I would feel some empathy. But I am simply a big person—who has been belittled and shamed for years—and so I take pleasure in it and make sure to flash a princess smile and wave her way.

"Three . . . two . . . one."

"Good evening, America!" Doc announces with flair. "It is almost nine p.m. on the East Coast and six p.m. here in the West. You have just watched the fascinating journey so far that has been Emery Jackson and her family. There they sit on the Friends & Family Couch."

Doc struts over to the couch.

"As you all saw tonight, Emery has a sister, Angel. She's an aspiring TV host. So let's get to know her a little bit better." Doc gently helps her to her feet. "So, Angel, how does it feel to see your sister embarking on the journey of a lifetime?"

Doc sticks the microphone a few inches from her mouth, but no words come out. She just stares at the camera like a raccoon caught poking through the garbage with a flashlight in its face. Angel, who has fake-baked so much in preparation for her national TV debut that she's oranger than a Highland Beach sunset looks skyward, trying to think of something to say. She's the one who needs a teleprompter.

The headset-clad stage director moves his finger in a circle and mouths to "move on."

"She's speechless, America," Doc transitions. "Downright speechless! The moment has taken her breath away. Can you really blame her?"

Angel sinks back into the couch and Dad rubs her back as Doc returns to reading the prompter.

"We also met Angel's parents, Jasper and Brandi," he says, kneeling beside them on the couch. "Jasper, you played professional basketball back in the day. Didn't quite make it on the NBA All-Star team, but as a minor leaguer you were the highest scorer in history for the Fresno Farmers. So you know a thing or two about achieving goals."

"I do," Dad boasts, somehow oblivious to just how damn condescending Doc is toward him. "There is no such thing as impossible."

Doc puts his hand on mom's thigh and adds, "And well, you two must be very proud of your daughter."

"Yes, of course, Angel is a special—"

"Emery," Mom interrupts with an elbow to Dad's ribs.

"Of course, Emery, yes, she is very brave," Dad says. "We love her no matter what."

"Well, it is quite an overwhelming night for the Jackson family and for all of us," Doc goes on. "If you aren't hooked, then you mustn't be a human being. Capping off things, we will end tonight's show just how we will end every Sunday show between now and January 19: with a weigh-in. Yes, that's right. Emery will bravely, boldly climb atop this here scale and reveal what progress—or lack thereof—she has made in her quest to lose fifty pounds in fifty days. But tonight we will first do something special. We will introduce to you Team Fifty. That is, the amazing team of professionals we have recruited to help Emery achieve a goal that, if accomplished, will mark the most dramatic weight loss in TV history. What you will be watching is not a reality show; it is what we call a Help Show. We are helping Emery, her family, and millions of YOU, people who just want to lead a life of physical freedom, to win your fight against fat."

As I stand next to the scale, from the kitchen walks in Team 50 in matching red, white, and blue Freedom tracksuits. They line up on the opposite side of the scale from me. It takes me a second to get that the *F* stitched on the chest of their jackets stands for Freedom and not Fat.

"Emery's nutritionist, celebrity diet guru Jackie Frank. Jackie has helped some of Hollywood's biggest stars slim down in a hurry. *TV! News* has called her 'the worst thing to happen to fat since the invention of liposuction.' Jackie, who boasts a body fat percentage of 2.3, is also the *New York Times*–bestselling author of *How to Eat without Actually Eating*."

Jackie shakes my hand and takes her position.

"Next up, we have Team Fifty's head athletic trainer, Derek Dodd. Derek, or 'Double D' or 'DD,' is a three-time Olympic medalist in the high jump, fifty-meter sprint, and the javelin. Over the course of his career as a trainer, he has eliminated a total of 4,567 pounds of fat from his clients. He's also known as playing the body double in the hit movie *Speedo Steve*."

"Last, but certainly not least, we have Dr. Genevieve Brisson. A major highlight of *Fifty Pounds to Freedom* will be seeing Emery undergo intensive psychotherapy aimed at uncovering the root causes of her obesity and hopefully helping her learn a new way to think about food, her body, her life, and her overall health. Perhaps you, the viewer, will also gain more insights into your own psychology. A member of France's prestigious board of psychology, Dr. Gen operates a successful practice based in Beverly Hills, London, and Paris. And yes, guys, the bilingual babe is single!"

My first impression of Dr. Gen is that she is too attractive to be a credible doctor. My experience with doctors, even head-shrinking ones, is that they're not very attractive people. Smart, yes. But not hot.

Long, dark hair cascades past her shoulders and her face looks flawless. The second thing I notice is that she has a calm to her that I like.

"So, America, this is Team Fifty!" Doc tells the camera. "But finally, to the reason we are all here. The star of our show, Emery Jackson." Doc motions for me with his stick mic. "Come here, Emery."

I step forward.

"How do you feel?" he asks.

"Nervous," I reply. "And hungry."

"This, of course, is the beginning of your weight loss journey," Doc says. "How did you spend it?"

"Honestly?"

"Indeed."

"I ate a lot of food."

"Starting tomorrow you will not be doing that," he says, draping his arm around my neck. "Don't worry, we have a team to help you, so there is nothing to be afraid of."

"There is nothing to fear but fat itself," Derek Dodd blurts.

"Well, then." Doc guffaws. "With that, let's do the weigh-in, shall we?"

Suddenly the lights dim except for the spotlight shining on the scale in the middle of our living room. A dramatic *dun-dun-dunnnnn* booms from a speaker. I'm shaking so much underneath my robe that my knees are knocking. I look at Ben over on the couch. He mouths *I love you* and smiles.

I think about what I can do with the money, how that will certainly make all this absurdity worth it. I also think about how sick and tired I am of being invisible to the world. I think about that foreclosure letter. I think about how I could stand to lose weight. And I think about Ben, who makes it all seem okay.

When I drop the robe to the floor I hear more than a few gasps from those gathered in the room. I'm not talking the kind of gasps people make when they see a Victoria's Secret model walk the runway in her sexy underwear. Rather, I'm talking the kind of gasps usually reserved for when Grandma craps herself at brunch.

I cringe as I slowly glance down over my boobs, which are pushed together so tightly I look like I have a butt on my chest. But this sight is far from gasp worthy. My gaze crawls downward to find what must have caused the breath to be taken out of the crowd. I realize that my lower stomach—an actual fit person might call them "abs"—is draped over the front of my bikini bottom so far that you can't even see that I'm wearing bottoms.

"Don't worry, guys." I turn around to show my butt. "See, I'm wearing bottoms."

I think it's funny, but a few in the crowd gasp—again.

Having already lost any ounce of shame I may have retained going into this event, I just shrug my shoulders and proceed to place one foot, then another, on the scale and watch as the numbers climb continually faster. I sneak a peek out of my left eye and see in giant white numbers: 199.2 lbs.

I have gained seven pounds since my visit with Dr. Hung over the summer. Not so bad, I think to myself as I rush to put my robe back on, as if millions of people didn't just see it and haven't thrown up a little in their mouths at the sight.

Doc turns to Derek Dodd. The muscle man shakes his head in disgust as he pushes buttons on his phone. "So, Double D, what's your take on this number. This one hundred ninety-nine?"

"Well, Doc," he continues, "according to my patented DD Body Mass Index Calculator™, being that Emery is five foot six, this gives her a BMI of 32.1. This, unfortunately, puts Emery above the ninety-fifth percentile for her age."

"For people like me for whom math is a four-letter word, what does this mean?" Doc asks.

"This makes her, in clinical terms, obese. Very dangerous territory. But I prefer to call it 'unhealthy.' I don't like to label people. But the bottom line is that it puts her at higher risk for diabetes, heart disease, depression, certain cancers, and a host of other ailments both big and small. And, of course, it will limit her socially, as it is a well-known fact that thin people find more success in life—in love, in business, in even getting a seat at a restaurant, you name it—than heavy people. That being said, if we can get Emery down below one hundred fifty pounds, she will then be in the upper range of a 'healthy' weight and, if anything, be on the road to a better, more fulfilling life. It is a worthy goal. Just how realistic of a goal it is will be up to Emery."

He glares across the scale at me slouching in shame. I don't know what is weirder: me just stepping on a scale in a two-piece bikini in front of America or listening to an "expert" talk about me as if I was a farm animal at a livestock auction.

"There you have it, Team Fifty," Doc says. "You all will have your work cut out for you. And America will be watching. Speaking of America . . . all of you please click on to Emery's YouTube channel throughout the week and connect with us on Twitter. Good night from Highland Beach, California. I'm Doc Harris and this has been *Fifty Pounds to Freedom*!"

MONDAY, DECEMBER 2 (DAY 1)

Boom, boom, boom.

At first it sounds like a muffled thud. Then it becomes clear it is a hard knock. Then comes a louder series of hard knocks.

Klak, klak, klak!

"Gimme a few." I groan.

I bury my head face first back under my pillow. Make. It. Stop.

"You've got thirty seconds, Emery," a male voice shouts from the other side of my bedroom door.

I click on my phone and rub my eyes. It's 6:02 a.m. I wiggle to my side and step down off the bed. My right knee cracks as I put weight on it. At what age is it cool to get a knee replacement?

"We're coming in, Emery!" the guy announces. "Here we come!"

I'm standing next to my baggy white T-shirt and sweatpants when Derek Dodd, decked out in black-and-white camouflage shorts and a tight-fitting white TEAM 50 shirt with red and blue trim, bursts through the door with a cameraman over his back shoulder.

"Do you know what today is?" he asks.

"Um, Monday?"

"No!" he barks. "It is Day 1 of your new life. It is Day 1 of creating the New-and-Improved Emery™. So get your workout clothes on and meet us in the dining room. You've got ten minutes. Boo-ya!"

Now. Something you need to know about me is that I am the kind of person who likes to wake up gradually. Mom and Dad call me "lazy," but I prefer "late bloomer." Secondly, you should know that I utterly despise trainers who talk like they are marine boot-camp instructors. It is about as annoying as the way Angel looks in any reflective surface (spoons, mirrors, shiny anythings) to check herself out. So DD's whole "boo-ya" silliness is not gonna cut it with me.

After suiting up, I head down and Jackie Frank, nutritionist extraordinaire, is at the table, on which sits a sad little assortment of bowls and plates.

"Good morning, Emery," Jackie greets me way too cheerily for someone at 6:15 a.m. "This here is the breakfast of a champion."

Jackie motions with her obnoxiously cut arms to each item and explains what each is, as if I have never seen "healthy" food before:

- One cup of oatmeal;

- One cup of fat-free cottage cheese;

- One apple;

- Seven different vitamins and supplements; and

- One glass of water.

"You see," Jackie begins. "In order to achieve your goal, you will have to lose an average of one pound a day. In a normal program, a person loses, at most, three pounds a week. You can only achieve this through two means: high-intensity workouts with Derek and total dedication to a low-calorie diet. We are going to keep you under 1,300 calories a day. And that's where I come in. There will be no cheating. You will be held accountable."

Just when I'm starting to wonder whether I signed up for a reality show or I am serving a sentence in food prison, Jackie lifts a box up from the kitchen floor and dumps its contents on the table in front of me. A stash of cookies, candy bars, potato chips, doughnuts, and a prized York Peppermint Pattie scatter across the table. There are bags of chips I don't even remember hiding.

"Did you guys hire the FBI or something?" I ask.

"No, but we did do a thorough sweep of this house, Emery. And as you can see here, we found all your food stashes. This kind of hoarding and hiding of food is very common. We see it with a lot of our clients. But if we are going to succeed at this, you and I can't have any secrets between us."

Jackie steps closer.

"So now that everything is literally out on the table, is there anything else you want to tell me?"

I consider confessing that I've already texted Ben to sneak me over a Bacon Double Cheeseburger for lunch, but I don't want to look like too much of a big fat pig, so I politely say "nope" and carefully scoop a spoonful of oatmeal into my mouth that is about as tasty as a mouthful of pillow stuffing.

"Could I have a dash of brown sugar? Just a teensy-weensy dash?" I ask Jackie with a grimace.

As the camera zooms closer to my misery face, Jackie sits down beside me.

"Filling your body with the empty calories of saturated fats and sugars is the Old Emery. The New Emery savors the natural flavor of whole grains, appreciates the goodness of a healthful meal. From now on, just think different about your food and your food will taste different."

"Differently," I correct her. "It's an adverb, because it is describing an action. You used an adjective instead."

"Huh?"

"Forget it."

I reluctantly go back to eating my breakfast, though I have to pinch my nose to get the cottage cheese down my throat without hurling. Jackie, at last, looks pleased.

"This, more or less, will be your daily diet for the next fifty days," she adds, placing a piece of paper in front of me on the table.

I stare at it, looking for any actual good food. There is none.

"Whatever happened to four-course meals?"

"Four-course meals, or any number of multicourse meals, were started hundreds of years ago in Europe, before we knew what we now do about healthy eating," Jackie lectures. "Multicourse meals were meant to be reserved for celebrations, special occasions. But, of course, Americans have turned it into a chance to eat like gluttonous pigs."

"So this is it? Why not just feed me bread and water?"

"Well, bread is carbs, so no. We will change it up here and there, but I believe in consistency. It might seem hard to believe right now, but by the end of this journey you will be craving this kind of food. I'm calling it your 'Freedom Menu™.'"

Breakfast:

1 cup plain instant oatmeal

1 slice of protein-rich multigrain bread

1 tablespoon jelly or jam

1 Apple/Orange/Banana

Snack:

5 mini-carrots with hummus

Lunch:

1 cup cooked regular rice pasta (gluten-free)

½ cup kidney, garbanzo, pinto, or white beans

Diced tomato

1 cup black bean soup or low-sodium chicken broth

Snack:

½ cup fat-free Greek yogurt

Dinner:

1 whole wheat tortilla

5 ounces chicken breast

Chopped tomatoes or onions

1 ounce fat-free cheese

Fifteen minutes after I finish "breakfast," I'm standing on the beach at the downtown Highland pier, where I am met by Derek "Double D" Dodd and a tall chick in butt-hugging shorts and a sports bra that looks a lot like my sister, because, as I get closer, it is, in fact, my sister.

"What's she doing here?" I ask Derek.

"A vital element of the Double D Power Program™ is competition. Not only do we exercise, but we also compete. Angel is here to spark that competition, to push you to be your best."

He leads us in some stretching, where I learn that I can't even friggin' touch my toes . . . unless I bend my knees.

"No bending the knees!" DD suddenly barks. "Keep them legs straight and breathe into the stretch." Let's just say the cameraman behind me is lucky I'm wearing sweatpants and not that bikini from last night's weigh-in.

"Okay, let's do this!" Double D starts jogging along the water's edge and orders us to keep up beside him. "Lift those knees up." I would liken DD's coaching strategy to a Marine Corps drill sergeant, but that would make DD seem too polite and gentle. I should decide to nickname DD the more appropriate "DL," as in "Douche Lord." But I choose to be nice. You know, for America.

As Angel gallops like a gazelle across the moist sand, my feet twist and turn with each step. A minute into the jog, I start falling back behind them, and another minute later I am already a good twenty yards behind them. A cameraman on an ATV rolls next to me, capturing my pathetic blob of humanity. I start to blow the hair off my face and realize there's sand stuck to my lips.

Sergeant Silly doubles back to me. "Meet us at the next lifeguard tower. You can do this. Now!"

I look ahead into the misty distance and see a lifeguard tower that looks to be about a mile away and think *there is no way in hell I can do this*. Fifteen minutes later, however, after running and walking and resting and then running some more, I do reach the tower. And immediately collapse onto my stomach. When I accidentally suck a grain of sand into my wheezing lungs, I begin coughing uncontrollably.

"Angel, go ahead and jog back to the pier," DD tells her. "We will meet you there."

DD kneels beside me and squirts water into my mouth like I'm a hamster. "You know what you're feeling right now?" he asks, rather unsympathetically.

"Like death?" I ask.

"No," he commands. "You're feeling the effects of years of inactivity, of lying in bed and watching TV, of sitting in front of a computer or staring at your phone for hours on end. You know how many calories you burn texting someone?"

I shake my head no.

"Approximately two calories an hour," he says. "Now guess how many calories you burn if you simply walked while texting?" He disgustedly shakes his head at my blank stare. "Let me tell you: three hundred calories."

The dude wipes some spit off his chin because he's frothing over all this silliness.

"The good news is that you're only sixteen and there is plenty of time to turn your life around. The bad news is that you are only thirty minutes into Day One of a fifty-day program. And so . . ." The muscle head lifts me to my feet from the armpits. "If any of this is going to do you any good, you gotta keep your heart rate up for an hour. Let's get back to the pier. Now."

If I could breathe, I would make some sort of snarky remark, but since I can't breathe, I just comply and somehow make it back to the pier huffing and puffing the entire mile.

"Where's Angel?" I ask DD.

"Out there." He points to the ocean. "She's swimming around the pier."

Poor girl, I think. Not only is the ocean cold this time of year, but that's far.

"That Angel is a real go-getter!"

"And you?" DD stands with his hands on his hips.

"You've got to be joking," I say. "I can't swim around the pier. That's insane. I can barely stand here without fainting right now. Plus I don't have a swimsuit."

Doc walks up from behind me and drops a pair of shorts and a wet suit at my feet. "Now you do, darling." He turns to the cameraman. "Why are you all just looking at me? Action!"

To say that swimming around that pier was quite possibly the hardest thing I've ever done would be accurate. But it also felt good to be able to do it, even though I basically doggy paddled the entire way.

I sit on a bench and pull my phone from my sweatpants pocket and see that it is not quite 8:30 a.m. The sun is barely peeking over the rooftops of the beachside mansions. There is no way I can survive a full day of this torture.

Back at home, a schedule is awaiting me, taped onto the refrigerator, which is now padlocked, lest this beast bust in and commandeer some calories.

EMERY'S DAILY TRAINING SCHEDULE:

6:00 a.m.	Wakeup
6:15 a.m.	Breakfast
7:00–8:00 a.m.	Beach Cardio
9:00 a.m.	Snack
9:30–10:30 a.m.	Yoga
11:00 a.m.–NOON	Therapy with Dr. Gen
NOON–1:00 p.m.	Lunch
2:00–3:00 p.m.	Weight Training/Body Sculpt
3:00 p.m.	Snack
4:00–5:00 p.m.	Trainer's Choice
6:00 p.m.	Dinner
7:00 p.m.	Home School/Blogging/Interviews
10:00 p.m.	Lights Out

I read the schedule line by line, trying to imagine myself doing this for one day, let alone fifty straight days. And I can't.

DAY 1 VIDEO BLOG
GIRLS DON'T NEED LONG HAIR

I am going to post videos here every now and then. I will come and talk about different things. Today I want to talk about hair.

Girls love their hair. From the time we are little girls, we are given dolls and tiny brushes that we use to comb long strands of princess locks. The dolls never have bobs or short buzz-like cuts. The message is that in order to be beautiful, hair must be long. But this fact also makes true another fact: Girls also HATE their hair.

No girl I've ever met actually thinks she has beautiful hair. It is always too straight, too curly, too thin, too wavy, too dark, or too light. I also will go out on a totally unscientific limb and guesstimate that approximately 97 percent of girls think their forehead is too big. Bangs were invented for this reason: to hide our foreheads. That's right, almost every girl thinks her forehead makes her look like an alien.

Just like nearly every other girl, I have bought into this long-hair myth. As I've gotten fatter and fatter, I have become even more attached to my hair because I have noticed that, no matter how massive I get, my hair doesn't get any bigger. It has been the one thing on my body that I am not disgusted to look at in the mirror.

The primary biological purpose of human hair is heat insulation. It keeps our bodies from losing too much heat. Our version of fur. But modern-day humans don't need hair. We have clothes!—you know, stuff to put on our bodies to keep warm.

Some people have floated the theory that females have evolved to grow their hair long in order to attract mates. Problem: There's no proof that is true at all. I think it is a total self-invented myth. And the real reason we tell ourselves we need so much hair on our heads, and that we need to obsess over it and spend insane amounts of money caretaking it, is because, well, every other chick does it. I think being beautiful is something that we decide to be true. It is not a born fact but an acquired truth created by society—meaning collectively by all of us!

And so today I got to thinking something "next level" about all of this hair business. I had a rough day. I exercised more today than I have probably in my entire life while concurrently eating the least. I'm so tired, I can barely lift my arm right now. Look. Anyway, that is how tired I am. And as

I ran on the beach, swam in the ocean, did yoga, lifted weights, all I could think was, "Gosh, I wish I didn't have this sweaty mass of hair stuck on my head."

So that is when I got to thinking: What if we all decided that being buzz cut is hot? What if every girl grabbed a pair of scissors and a razor and just hacked off all her hair? The answer is that it would be totally awesome. Everyone might start doing it. It would be the hair equivalent of a Martin Luther King march. We would all band together and declare freedom from our hair cuffs! I mean, obviously guys are ten steps ahead of us on this. At some point in history, men decided that men with long hair were either hippies or just trying to cover up bald spots with a bad comb-over.

Now, it is easy for me to sit here and say all this into a laptop cam. It is another thing to actually DO something about it. So today, here in my first video, I am going to do something about it.

Here in my hand is a pair of clippers. I took them from my dad's drawer. With these, I am going to do what every girl has thought about doing at some point in their lives, but was probably too scared to do. Today made me realize that now is the time to be the change I want to be. That is why my hair will now find freedom. And it is my hope that if you agree with me, you will do the same.

WEDNESDAY, DECEMBER 4 (DAY 3), 1:34 A.M. PST

This is what you think about constantly when one day you go from being an obese teenager enjoying a 4,000-calorie-a-day diet to within a few days being the subject of a sick and twisted reality TV experiment suffering through a deprivation diet:

Food Food Food Food Food Food Food Food Food Food Food
Food Food Food Food Food Food Food Food Food Food Food
Food Food Food Food Food Food Food Food Food Food Food
Food Food Food Food Food Food Food Food Food Food Food
Food Food Food Food Food Food Food Food Food Food Food
Food Food Food Food Food Food Food Food Food Food Food
Food Food Food Food Food Food Food Food Food Food Food
Food Food Food Food Food Food Food Food Food Food Food
Food Food Food Food Food Food Food Food Food Food Food
Food Food Food Food Food Food Food Food Food Food Food
Food Food Food Food Food Food Food Food Food Food Food
Food Food Food Food Food Food Food Food Food Food Food

Food Food Food Food Food Food Food Food Food Food Food
Food Food Food Food Food Food Food Food Food Food Food
Food Food Food Food Food Food Food Food Food Food Food
Food Food Food Food Food Food Food Food Food Food Food
Food Food Food Food Food Food Food Food Food Food Food
Food Food Food Food Food Food Food Food.

Oh, and when you're dreaming: more food. And when the dream wakes you up and you're lying in bed unable to fall back asleep because you're starving: even more food.

This. Totally. Sucks.

THURSDAY, DECEMBER 5 (DAY 4)

No matter how many brain cells I kill from starvation, there are three days in my life I know for sure I will never forget.

A) The day in sixth grade when my father told me I could look more skinny, like my sister for example, if I simply "laid off the snacks." I immediately decided I would never, ever again do what he told me to do.

B) The day when I was nine and I found out how babies were really made and was so distraught I couldn't look my parents in the eye for like a month.

C) And today.

Today started off normal enough. I woke up at six, ate some awful "food," popped seven giant vitamins, jogged on the beach, got yelled at by DD for not getting down deep enough on my lunges, ate some more tasteless food, sat in an hour-long therapy session with Dr. Gen as she tried to get me to "open up," had some serious daydreams about cheeseburgers and french fries, and lifted weights until my arms felt like they were going to fall off my body.

It is Day Four of the reality show and the only particularly interesting things thus far were that A) Last night was the first Wednesday show airing and B) I was loving not having hardly any hair on my head.

But when I checked the video I had posted three days ago, I saw it had apparently caught on, having already racked up thirty-four million views.

Below the video player were a list of more than a thousand (mostly supportive) comments:

I love you, Emery!

You go, girl!

Hair = Sucks . . . so totally right hahaha

You are beautiful no matter what they say.

Your sister is so hot. I wanna have her.

Preach the truth, sistah!

You look fatter without hair FYI

I want to be you, Emery!

Emery for president!

I don't watch TV anymore but this video makes me want to watch your TV show! You are so inspiring.

My friends and I just had a hair-shaving party!

The comments went on and on. And on.

After dinner, Angel, Mom, Dad, and I go to the movies. Doc wants to get some footage of us "in real life" and not just centered on eating and exercising, so we go to the FilmLight Cineplex up on Coastal Highway.

The smell of the buttery popcorn hits me the second I walk into the lobby. With nonstop Food Police watching me, and with Jackie throwing away all my secret stashes, I managed not to eat any junk food all week. But I also hadn't yet been bombarded with the oozing fantasticality of movie theater popcorn. My heart is racing. My mouth drools. I want it. Real bad.

As my family stands in line for tickets, I fish out my phone and call Jackie. She had instructed me to call her "in case of emergency"—and this was certainly one—like some sort of suicide hotline.

"Jackie"—I panic while staring at the glass box of popcorn, watching it cascade down into a fluffy pile of yumminess—"I'm at the movies and I want popcorn, like really want popcorn." I am nearly hyperventilating. "I don't think I can stop myself. I just need to have one small popcorn. That's all. I won't put extra butter on it, no salt, and I promise I will work out extra hard tomorrow."

"Don't do it, Emery!" Jackie orders me. "Even a small popcorn has six hundred seventy calories, not to mention thirty-four grams of fat and eighty grams of carbs. That is just too many. You've got your next weigh-in coming up in three days. You need to do what I say. Hear me, Emery? You need to take yourself out of that situation. You aren't ready—"

I hear her but I'm not listening. The exploding yellow kernels have cast a spell on me, and I am shuffling toward the food counter as if drawn by gravity. Without saying good-bye, I hang up the phone and keep walking.

"Excuse me." A heavyset girl in pigtails is suddenly standing between me and my popcorn. "Excuse me!"

Behind Lil' Ms. Excuse Me lurks a few of her girlfriends, all around high-school age. Just when I am about to bitch-slap them out of my way, she adds, "I am so sorry to bother you, but we noticed that camera over there following you and, um, we were wondering . . . are you Emery Jackson?"

"Uh, yeah." Her question snaps me out of my stupor. "I am Emery Jackson. Do I know you?"

"I knew it!" The girl squeals and hops up and down like a pogo stick. "It really is you!"

"In the flesh." I am a bit confused. "And, um, how do I know you?"

"We love your show. And, obvi, your video about how stupid long hair is was so amazing. We were just talking about how we want to throw a head-shaving party and donate all the hair to a cancer charity. You are so amazing, Emery. We all love you."

"Well, thanks," I say. "You're so kind. But why do you *love* me?"

"Because you're so real and cool and honest," she says. "Can we get a picture with you? *Pleeeease?*"

By now, Angel, Mom, and Dad have come over to witness the worship session. The girl hands Angel her phone and asks, "Can you take our picture, please?"

Angel glances at the girl's phone as if it's a big stinky pile of dog poo and with a faux-polite smile says, "No. Sorry."

As Angel stomps off into the theater, the fangirl shrugs and instead finds a stranger to take it. "Emery sandwich, girls!"

"Emery Jackson?" Another girl taps me on my shoulder. "*The* Emery Jackson?"

It's Kendra, Highland High's alpha Beautiful Girl. "Well, look at you! Loving the show. Hello! I didn't realize you were doing, like, a *real* TV show. That is so amazing, Emery. I know you are gonna win it. I have always believed in you. Even when you were kind of a hot mess. I always believed in you."

"Thanks, I think."

"It's true," she insists.

"Let's get inside, the movie is starting!" Angel whines, tugging on my Mom's arm.

Kendra sidles up next me. "Let's take a selfie!"

Spotting me, yet another gaggle of girls comes up to me. Being the kind of big-time celebrity who cares about her fans, I take pics with them.

And as the group of fans walks away giggling, I realize why today is one of the most memorable ever: It is the day that I realize that I am famous.

FRIDAY, DECEMBER 6 (DAY 5)

"I'm afraid to say this, but this isn't really working for me—or you." Dr. Gen drops her notepad down on the coffee table between us. "This is our fifth therapy session and you still refuse to open up."

"Isn't that your job, to get me to open up? And as a patient, isn't it my job to resist, to want to remain in my blissful state of denial? Seems to me that I am doing my job, and you're not doing yours."

Dr. Gen takes a deep inhale and lets it out. It takes a big, fat brat to make such a patient, calm person lose her cool. "Therapy is a two-way street," she explains in her French accent. "It is a relationship. And like any functional relationship there is a mutual dynamic at play. What if we were playing a game of tennis?"

"I hate tennis."

"Then it is a perfect example. Let's say you are supposed to be playing tennis against someone, but because you hate the sport, you just stand there and go through the motions. But meanwhile your opponent is doing everything they can to compete and get the most out of the experience. You wouldn't have much of a game would you? Well, that is exactly what is happening between us in this room. I can only ask questions. It is up to you to open up and give honest answers. This just isn't working."

"Your analogy is flawed."

"Okay, tell me why."

"Because unlike in tennis, as a therapist you aren't supposed to be my opponent. You're supposed to be on my team. On my side."

"So do you feel like I'm not on your side?"

"Kind of."

"Why?"

"Because I feel like just because I am fat, you're assuming something is wrong with me, that you are prejudging me before I have even said a single word. In that sense, you are just like every other person in my life. And actually, that is kind of rude— especially from someone who is supposed to help me. I don't care if you are a French shrink, speak ten languages, and have written bestselling books."

I get up from my chair and walk over to the far corner and point at a fish-eye lens of a camera on the ceiling. "And this camera here. It doesn't exactly make me feel like I can trust you."

"Would it make you feel better if we turned the cameras off?"

"Duh, of course."

The door to the room suddenly swings open and in bounds Doc.

"Cut! Cut! Cut! Apologies for interrupting," he says. "But we cannot turn off these cameras, my friends. It's in the contract that we can film everything."

"Then I'm not quote-un-quote opening up," I hastily reply. "The contract only says I will attend daily therapy sessions. It doesn't require me to do anything else in this room."

Doc ponders my point. "Fine," he relents. "We will stand down for five minutes, let you two talk privately, but then the cameras come back on. Everyone, take five."

"In French," Dr. Gen explains, "we call what we are a doing a *tête-à-tête*. What you would call a private conversation between two people. So, Emery, can I be totally honest with you? Can we have an honest tête-à-tête?"

"Please do," I say. "That actually would be refreshing."

"Look," Dr. Gen starts. She takes off her black-frame secretary glasses. "I don't blame you for not trusting me, and for not opening up. I am going to level with you. The reason I am here is not because Doc wants me here. In fact, I was told he wanted the third Team Fifty member to be a life coach, not a psychotherapist. But I am on this show as your therapist because Lana, as president of THE NETWORK, wanted me to be a part of this. In fact, she wouldn't green light the series until Doc agreed to feature you in therapy. Because she wants others to learn that fixing someone on the outside starts with fixing someone on the inside."

"And it makes for good TV," I add.

"Fair enough," she agrees.

"Okay, so why did they pick you? Was Dr. Drew unavailable?"

"Because, without breaching any client confidentiality, let's just say Lana is familiar with my work. I want to help you, Emery. Yes, these may not be ideal conditions, and it certainly isn't a setting I am used to either, but I think both of us can accomplish a lot of good in this room—for you and for a lot of other girls in similar states. But I can only knock. You are the only one who can open the door."

As if on cue, there's a knock on the door of the den. "We ready to roll again, ladies?" Doc asks through the door. "I've got a thirteen-person crew about to start into overtime and we gotta wrap. Let's get back to work!"

Dr. Gen and I exchange equally bemused glances. I nod yes.

"We're ready," she tells Doc.

"Okay, then," he says. "Action!"

Dr. Gen picks up her pad and pen from the table, crosses her legs, and rests her hands in her lap.

"So, Emery, how do you feel today?"

"Nervous."

"What are you nervous about?"

"Well, my next weigh-in is in two days."

"Why does that make you nervous?"

"Because I'm afraid that I won't have lost any weight. I am afraid that I will disappoint everyone."

"Would you be disappointed?"

"I honestly fear disappointing other people more than myself. I mean, I am okay with it, but I don't want to let my family down. And now, my fans."

"Do you think that your fear of disappointing others, especially your parents, has maybe kept you from trying to lose weight in the past?"

I think to myself for a few seconds. "Probably. But I'm also lazy."

"But from your performance so far this week, you just proved you are anything but lazy. You have done every workout, stuck to every bit of your diet. In fact, wouldn't you say you've been quite motivated?"

"Okay, yes, you are right." I smile. "You're good at this therapy stuff."

Dr. Gen smiles and says, "It's my job."

Gen calls our session a "breakthrough" and I do leave therapy feeling refreshed—and less nervous about Sunday's weigh-in.

As I'm walking downstairs for lunch, Doc catches up to me. "Great scene, Emery. Positively brilliant stuff."

"I try," I reply. "But, no offense, I'm doing this for myself, not for your stupid show."

Doc ignores my comment.

"Speaking of the show," Doc says. "Lana is waiting for us downstairs. She has some news for us."

When I enter the kitchen I am instantly met with applause. Lana and her two cronies I met with back at THE NETWORK headquarters last month are standing at the counter with wide smiles.

"The premiere of the show brought in three millions viewers, making it the highest series premiere in our network's twenty-year history," Lana gushes. "But that's not even the good news. We just got the numbers for the second episode on Wednesday night and, get ready for it, it brought in *eight* million viewers."

Lana is so peppy I fear she may pee herself. I am confused.

"And is that a lot of people?" I ask. "There are something like three hundred million people in the United States. So three million isn't, like, a lot."

"Emery, *Fifty Pounds* was the highest rated show in the history of THE NETWORK. We got a smash hit show on our hands!" Lana crosses her arms in front of her chest and sighs. "You have to remember something: People don't watch TV like they used to. That's why we usually have to trick people into watching our shows. You know, spend hundreds of thousands on marketing and ad campaigns and billboards, promising something that will shock or surprise them. But with your show we actually did the opposite. We just put it on the air. And people found it and loved it!"

"Wow, smashing, just smashing," Doc enthuses. "I am over the moon about this!"

"That's not all," Lana continues. "Fenton has some data on the show's social engagement."

Turns out that Mr. Hipster Guy from that THE NETWORK meeting, the one with the goatee, is named Fenton.

Fenton steps forward and reads off his iPad. "First of all, the YouTube channel we launched for you is a major hit. Emery's first video blog has gotten fifty millions views and counting. On the social media front, the official Facebook page now has eight hundred thousand 'likes' and Emery's Twitter account has 5.5 million followers."

"But I don't have a Twitter account," I interrupt. "I hate Twitter."

Fenton sheepishly looks to Lana.

"We started one for you," she says. "We knew you'd be too busy."

"Without my permission?" I ask.

"Technically," Doc butts in. "You did give us permission. In the contract."

"It's all working smoothly," Lana continues. "Fenton here has been ghost-tweeting for you. There is nothing to be concerned about. We want you focused on your weight-loss challenge. All these bells and whistles are fine and good, but without you committing all you have to losing the weight, we don't have a show. And last I checked, tweeting doesn't burn very many calories."

As Lana chuckles, Fenton hands me his device and shows me "my" Twitter page, on which "I" have posted a total of thirty-eight messages in the last week, among them:

> **@EmeryJax50** My feet are sore today, but these SneakerSwag kicks make them better.

> **@EmeryJax50** Thanks to #NaturalFoodSource for my yummy breakfast!

> **@EmeryJax50** Tune in tonight. I'm in a @SoCalBikini again!

"These aren't tweets," I tell them. "These are ads."

"These days," Fenton says, "there's no difference, honey. Celebrities tweeting for themselves is so 2010."

PLEASE YOURSELF, GIRLS!!!

Tomorrow's the big weigh-in. If you haven't heard, I have to get on a scale and find out if all of the running and jumping and starving I've been doing is making any difference in my personal meat department. To be honest, my body, while still by most appearances and angles looks very Jabba the Hutt–like, feels a little bit tighter, and maybe less flabby. I don't know. We'll see.

Today I don't want to talk about fat for a change. I want to tell you guys about something I thought about the other day when I was looking at some women's magazines in line at the grocery store. The covers were splashed with head-lines like "How to Please a Man," "How to Make Your Boyfriend Go Crazy in Bed," "Five Ways to Make Him Beg for More." And I came to realize that there wasn't a single headline about how a girl could actually make HERSELF happy or give HERSELF pleasure. Seriously. And these magazines are edited and written by women! It's like Gender Cannibalism.

Don't worry, I'm not going to tell you how and why you should pleasure yourself. I imagine you've already figured that out on your own. But there wasn't anything that said, "Okay, this is your birth canal and this is that little button above it, and this is how you can make it feel amazing." Nope. Instead it was all about how to talk dirty to turn on a guy, or how to wear trampy clothes.

First off, you ain't gonna be able to make anyone happy unless you first make sure YOU are happy. That's just a basic truth in life.

I am a quote whore, and I like one writer who really churned them out, Ralph Waldo Emerson. And if you can get over the fact that he has maybe the dorkiest name ever, you can appreciate the truth of which he speaks. My favorite quote of Waldo's: "Nothing can bring you peace but yourself. Nothing can bring you peace but the triumph of principles."

So, girls, this is my message to you: Stand up for and take care of yourself first.

When I was little, I used to get stuck in the car with my dad a lot, and he'd always be listening to some oldies station. Occasionally a good one would come on. And one song I loved had a line about how you can't please everyone so you have to take care of yourself.

So go please yourself. And, oh, stop buying those stupid women's magazines. I am.

SUNDAY, DECEMBER 8 (DAY 7)

My phone alarm goes off at 6:00 a.m.

The weigh-in is tonight.

The telltale sign that I am obsessed with something is that it is the first thing I think of when I wake up in the morning.

The weigh-in is tonight.

And I keep saying it over and over like a freakin' mental patient.

The weigh-in is tonight.

There I go again. Ugh. Make it stop!

Back when I started this "journey" an entire week ago, I really, truly, seriously, honestly did not care so much about losing the weight as I did about winning the money. The weight loss, to me, would serve as a means to justify the end I wanted, to allow me to live a life that would make me a lot happier than my current one. Sure, I had decided that I was gross and disgusting looking, but it didn't, like, mean the world to me to actually have to drop some pounds.

But just one week into this freak show, I am realizing that I really *do* want to lose the weight. It has become a test of my will, of my strength, of my ability to do something I set my mind to, something that will give me a sense of control.

Maybe it is because I am being challenged. Maybe it is because I now realize I have all these fans rooting for me. Maybe it is because THE NETWORK has agreed to pay me $1,000 for every pound I lose and $1 million if I lose fifty pounds in fifty days. Or maybe the truth is that I might be happier being a Not Fat Human. I don't even need to be skinny. I just don't want to be fat anymore. I am over it.

All I know is I am consumed with the thought that tonight I will get on the scale and in cold hard numbers on a screen, the entire world will see if I have succeeded or not. And I don't want to fail.

That is why I've decided I will eat half of what I normally do. Given that my normal diet these days is about a tenth of what I used to eat up until a week ago, that means I would eat about one-twentieth of my old diet. That's right: I am going to starve myself.

At breakfast, I eat half an apple, half the bowl of cottage cheese, and half my oatmeal.

"What's wrong?" Jackie asks.

"Just not hungry this morning," I lie.

Predictably, an hour later, by the end of my beach run I feel like I am going to pass out. But I manage to survive.

It's now five o'clock, an hour from showtime, and I have spent the last two hours teetering on the edge of sleep. Turns out, calories really do equal energy, because after cutting them in half I have none.

When I walk into my bedroom, Ryan is folding my robe and bikini and placing them onto my mattress with care. This isn't for the cameras. He's doing it to make my life easier, not something I can say anyone else is doing for me right now.

"You really got skillz, kid," I joke.

"Yeah, what can I say? Everyone has their calling," Ryan says. "Mine is organizing girls' clothes."

He quickly finishes up his task and I can totally picture him being one of those hot sales clerks at Abercrombie. No, make that one of the models. All he needs is a strand of hay stuck between his teeth and his shirt ripped off.

As I picture this loveliness, Ryan steps from the bed and makes a beeline for the door.

"Where you going?" I ask.

"Doc wants me to go help with the rehearsal."

"That guy is a ballbuster, eh?"

"Ballbuster? He's more like a ball-taker." Ryan lowers his voice to a hush. "I obviously have been totally emasculated doing this job. He's brilliant, but a total nut."

Ryan has longish sandy-blond hair that is perpetually falling in front of his eyes, forcing him to have to shake it off his face. In a sexy, masculine way. He's also got thick, broad shoulders and a narrow waist that almost certainly is from all the surfing he has told me he does in his free time. Yesterday at lunch, we had our first-ever conversation. I learned that he just turned nineteen, grew up in the Valley (I won't hold it against him that he's an Inlander), and dropped out of Santa Monica College two weeks ago just to PA on this show. His dream is to make documentaries, and Doc has convinced him this Fat Girl reality show is his route to that. Say what you want about Doc, the little prick has powers of persuasion.

Despite his poor career planning decision, I decide Ryan is cute.

He slides his hands in his jeans pockets and asks me, "You nervous?"

"Yeah, why? Is it obvious?"

"Well, you haven't really eaten all day. So I figured . . ."

Ryan would know. The guy has been with me all day and night for the last seven days.

"I admire you," he says. "It takes a lot of balls to do what you're doing."

"Yeah, Doc gave me your balls to borrow."

"You're the funniest girl I've ever met." Ryan giggles. His smile exposes a sweet set of dimples and a perfectly straight set of white teeth. I catch myself fantasizing that if I weren't three times his size and didn't look like a cow in a bikini, maybe actually kissing him would be a possibility.

"Okay, I better get down there," he says nervously. He stares at the floor for a beat in deep thought, then looks up at me.

"Is something wrong?" I ask him.

"No," he replies. "Everything's fine. Good luck tonight."

Ryan flashes an unconvincing half smile and leaves.

Minutes later, when I slip into my bikini—the "slimming" black one—it doesn't feel as tight on my body as last week, especially in the gut/ass region. Maybe I have dropped some pounds, after all. But I wouldn't know because they have taken every scale out of my house and forbade me from stepping on one except for the live weigh-in every Sunday. But I can tell the suit is fitting looser. So all that cardio and nuts and berries and low-carb dinners may be working. Either that or I just stretched them out during last week's weigh-in, which, let's face it, is the most likely reason.

Knock, knock.

I know that gentle knock.

"Come in, Bennigan!"

My bear of a boyfriend is standing in the doorway holding a bouquet of red roses. A cameraman stands a few feet behind him in the hallway.

"Oh, Benny," I say, wrapping my arms around his thick waist. "Wrong show."

I take them anyway, and inhale the aroma. Ben bounds into the room with his gawky Big Bird strut and sits down on my bed. He's wearing a flannel shirt, untucked to let his giant belly relax freely.

"I'm proud of ya," he says. "I don't care what the scale says tonight. I just want you to know I love you no matter how many pounds you are, no matter what any haters might say."

"What haters?" I ask.

"I don't know, like, just stupid people on the Web and stuff," he fumbles. "I don't mean anyone in particular."

"C'mon, Ben," I press. "What's being said out there? You can tell me. I'm a big girl—pun intended."

"Okay, Em. All right." He lowers his voice to a whisper, as if the microphone clipped to his shirt won't capture his words, and as if Doc and his minions won't subtitle his whispers anyway. "No one thinks you're going to be able to lose the weight. They think you're way in over your head with this whole thing."

"Who is 'no one'? Tell me, Ben."

"Your family, for starters," he says.

"Wow, news flash! My family doesn't believe in me. Tell me something that isn't more obvious." I won't admit it, but now my blood pressure has risen. I'm annoyed. "What are they saying?"

"I just overheard your mom downstairs talking to your nutritionist, telling her that you're sneaky when it comes to food, that you're probably snacking behind their backs."

"Did you defend me?"

"I couldn't. I wasn't supposed to be listening in the first place."

"But you know that's not true," I fume. "I mean, I did ask you for a cheeseburger on Day One, but thanks to you, I never got one. Otherwise, I've been really good. Man, that really pisses me off, though. What else did they say?"

"Nothing, really," Ben insists.

I give him my "tell the truth or I will inflict misery" glare.

"Aw, c'mon. Emery." He is rendered disabled by my powers. "Fine. Well, Angel just told Doc that she thinks you'd be more motivated if you had to do all your beach workouts in a bikini. She also said she would be more than happy to train alongside you in every session—you know, as motivation."

He steps closer. "That's why I came up here to tell you. I love you too much. Everyone just saw them saying all this on TV. You deserve to know. It's the right thing to do." He looks back over his shoulder at the cameraman kneeling in the corner shooting our "scene." "And I don't care if this is all on TV."

"Aw, Bennigan"—I sigh—"You're making me cry, which is great, because maybe I will lose some water weight." I wipe away a tear from my cheek. "You're seriously too sweet."

As we're hugging, Doc bounds into my bedroom. "Five

minutes, kids. Meet me downstairs." He gives us a double-cheesy thumbs-up and hustles out.

Downstairs, we all assume our positions. Ben and my family on the couch, my Team 50 coaches to the left of the scale, and me, robed like a flasher, to the right of it, with a tuxedoed Doc in the middle.

"Welcome back, America," Doc opens. "This is *Fifty Pounds to Freedom*. As you watch in your living rooms, we stand in the Jackson family's living room. The last week has been an awakening of sorts. We've seen Emery go from a sedentary sixteen-year-old to an energetic disciple of discipline. We've seen Emery go from being, in her words, 'invisible,' to being instantly one of the most famous teenagers in the country."

He walks slowly toward me, not taking his eyes off the camera. "And now comes the moment we find out if all that hard work, all that sacrifice, all that coaching is paying off."

"Emery, how do you feel?"

"Like I want to get this over with!" I say.

"Understandable, darling. Totally understandable." He steps away in the direction of my family, who are sitting stone-stiff as if in church pews. "But before we do your weigh-in, we are going to throw in a little twist. Emery's goal is to lose fifty pounds in fifty days. And if she should lose the entire fifty in time, the Jackson family wins one million dollars."

Doc gestures to my fam. "Each of you, please stand up."

Ben, Mom, Dad, and Angel comply. Hesitantly. If they know what the hell Doc is up to, they sure are good actors.[8]

---

[8] In fifth grade, Angel and I entered a spelling bee. I won it by spelling "iguana." Angel, meanwhile, was booted in the first round when she spelled gravy "G-R-A-Y-V-E-E."

"Let's conduct a little poll," Doc tells them. "I'm going to ask each of you whether or not you believe Emery is on track to meet her goal. In other words, do you think Emery has lost seven pounds? Now the good news is that if you guess correctly, you will each get a thousand dollars. But should you guess wrong, well, that's the bad news: Ten thousand dollars will be deducted from the family's grand prize for each wrong answer."

If Mom and Angel didn't have layers of MAC Studio fix and bronzer and tinted moisturizer coating their faces, they'd have just turned as white as polar bears.

It is a loser move on Doc's part to ambush my family like this, but I'd be lying if I didn't admit that it's nice to see someone other than myself put in a pressure cooker.

Ryan rushes bent over toward Doc and, just off camera, hands him four white cardboard cue cards. Doc takes them and pulls a magic marker from his pocket.

"Rather than telling us your answer now, each of you will write YES or NO on these cards," Doc instructs the group, handing each a card. One by one, they discreetly scrawl their answers.

Doc takes the marker from Angel, who is seated on the far right, and tells them not to reveal their answers. He walks back to me at the scale.

"Okay, Emery," he says. "The moment that everyone has been waiting for: Your weigh-in." He looks back into the camera. "In one minute. After the break."

The second we cut into commercial, Mom gets up from the couch and bum-rushes Doc. "What's with this poll business?" she growls. "We never agreed to this. It's just so unprofessional. You could have at least given us a heads-up. It's just so unfair—"

"Darling," Doc interrupts. "We can discuss this afterward. Just remember, this *is* what all of you signed up for. It's a show. You're the talent. I'm the producer. We make the rules. You live by them."

"Back in ten!" barks the stage manager. "Nine, eight . . ."

Mom throws Doc a stink-face and sulks back to the couch, settling next to Dad. Though I stare them all down, Dad and Angel won't make eye contact with me and whisper among themselves.

"And we're back!" Doc announces. "Emery Jackson has been dieting, exercising, working hard toward her goal of fifty pounds in fifty days. This is Day Seven. Is she on pace to lose the weight? Will her family walk away with bonus money, or lose? We're about to find out."

The lights dim and the spotlight shines on me. This is my cue. I drop my robe. This time no gasps of sheer horror, just a hush comes over the room. You could cut the tension with a knife—you know, the kind you might use to slice up those delish french bread pizzas from Ralph's.

I step on the scale, the readout for which they have now placed directly over my head so that I can't see it.

The first thing I notice is a giant smile on Ben's face, followed by Doc reading the numbers. "189 pounds."

A pocket of air large enough to float the Goodyear blimp releases from my lungs as the room erupts in applause.

"Ten pounds, Emery," Doc says. "You've lost ten pounds! Positively smashing!"

Jackie, DD, and Dr. Gen rush over and group-hug me. "Congrats, babe," DD whispers. "Now you glad I made you swim the pier?"

"A first week success, a true accomplishment," Doc adds.

"And you're three pounds ahead of schedule."

I remain next to the scale, surrounded by my tracksuit-fitted Team 50, as Doc steps to the couch. "But," he says, "the question now is did Emery's family—and her boyfriend—believe in her?"

Doc asks them to stand.

"Time for their answers," he starts. "Jasper, you can go first."

Dad flips his card to reveal a YES and blows me a kiss across the room, the first sign of actual affection I can recall from him in the last six years.

"Oh, now," Doc reacts. "A proud papa, indeed."

"Now, Brandi, my dear." Mom grins nervously before revealing a giant YES.

Ben is next in line, but I know this answer even before he flips the card to show that he has written his loyal YES in giant block letters. He offers an adorable wink, which I reciprocate. The audience must be eating up the schmaltz.

"And finally we come to your sister, Angel," Doc says. "She has been with you, side by side, at your beach workouts every morning. Presumably, she would know how you're doing, right?"

"Presumably," I say into the mic. "You might assume so."

Angel isn't smiling. Yet she also isn't frowning. She's looking past me with a blank stare as she slowly flips her card to reveal her hand-scrawled NO.

Mom mouths *uh-oh* and puts her hand in front of her lips. Dad crosses his arms in front of his chest and looks downward. Doc points the mic back into my face.

"Well," he says. "Three out of four of your support team believed in you. But your sister's miscalculation has cost you all ten thousand dollars."

The living room lay silent but for the hum of the portable studio lights flanking either side of the room. "So, Emery. What do you have to say?"

I yank the microphone from Doc's hand and say, "Fuck you, Angel."

LET'S TALK ABOUT THE REAL F-BOMB

I thought they had a seven-second delay. I seriously did.

Needless to say, there was the inevitable Twitter campaign and Facebook page started by appalled citizens demanding a Congressional inquiry into how such a thing could happen. The online campaign from the Family First Council to rid television of "the great Satan" that is *Fifty Pounds to Freedom*. And, of course, I've been scolded beyond scolding by my mom, dad, boyfriend, our producer, THE NETWORK, and my grandmother Dotty in Arizona, who apparently had to be rushed to the hospital after going into hysterics upon hearing the bomb drop. Not to mention my sister. She has vowed to never speak to me again.

Now I'm being pressured to say I am publicly sorry. So, pathetic apology coming in three, two, one. "I am so sorry if I offended anyone by my poor judgment in using a profane word. It was a mistake."

I respect the fact—right or wrong—that there are "dirty" words in our language, and every language for that matter, that describe dirty things and aren't to be said in public because, God knows, we don't want anyone to be exposed to dirty things any more than they already are in this dirty modern world of ours. That being said, there are more damaging words. I've been called a lot of downright hurtful things: Miss Piggy, Jelly Belly, Big Bertha, Large Marge, Bacon Boobs. And I have had the dishonor of being called all the cliché "muffin" nicknames, among them: Muffin Top, Muff-o-potamus, Muff-a-lo, Muffin Meat. And these are just the names I have heard said to my face. But the worst word that has ever been thrown at me by these Big People Bullies is "fat."

Most of my life I have been called fat—so much so that I started calling myself fat just so I could take ownership of what is, basically, a really hurtful adjective. The F-bomb itself is not a specific attack, an indictment of someone's appearance or personhood. It is just a word we have collectively deemed as a society to be "dirty" or "bad."

I'm not so naïve as to think I can convince the entire English-speaking world that the F-word should be taken off the Don't Utter on TV List. But I will step up, right here on my humble little video channel as I sit on my bed talking into my laptop, and propose that if we do keep the F-word in the protected species category, that we also add a second F-word. The one that is waaaay more damaging to people, especially young girls who are having a hard enough time trying to make it through life. That F-word, the one that is truly hurtful, is FAT. So the next time you drop this F-bomb, please think twice.

FRIDAY, DECEMBER 13 (DAY 12)

Doc is annoyed that actual reality is getting in the way of his supposed reality show and thus he's living his own personal Friday-the-Thirteenth nightmare.

"We must take these damn workouts indoors, back at the house in private," Doc announces to the crew gathered on the beach. "The paparazzi are getting out of control. This is no way to shoot a reality show."

Not realizing the absurdity of his statement, Doc cuts short my morning run with DD and my boob-a-licious running partner Angel Jackson.

"Look at those jackals." Doc points to a pack of photographers clustered a hundred yards away on the pier focusing down on me below. "This is what killed Diana. God rest her soul." A few of them have lenses so long they look like bazookas. "We pay a lot of money to get permits to shoot here," Doc complains to no one in particular. "Yet they come down here for free, unregulated. It's thoroughly unfair and impeding our production.

That's the problem with this country of yours: it is set up to accommodate the lowest common denominator—the rats, the cockroaches, the lazy bastards cheating the system." Doc looks around his group of techies and assistants and various hangers-on. "Where the hell is Ryan?"

"Here, sir," Ryan says, stepping forward.

"Take Emery back to the house in the van, *pronto*."

As Ryan hustles me into the white crew van along with a cameraman, a guy in a polo shirt and skinny jeans runs up to the car and knocks on my window. I flip the guy the bird.

"Gun it, Ry Guy," I say. "This pap is freaking me out."

"Please, stop!" The guy shouts through the passenger's side window. He starts running after the van. "I'm from THE NETWORK!"

Ryan hits the brakes. I roll down the window.

"Who are you?" I ask.

"Raymond Lopez," he answers out of breath. "I work for THE NETWORK. I'm your publicist."

He reaches into the van and shakes my hand. I look past him and see like seven photographers sprinting toward us snapping pictures.

"Get in!" I bark. When he does, Ryan guns it out of the parking lot.

"Buckle up, Mr. Lopez," Ryan says with a smirk as Raymond braces himself in the backseat.

He is beanpole thin and holding a murse in his lap. "Lana pulled me off *Screech Loves Jessie* to work your show. We've been inundated with media requests over the last few days. She thinks you need full-time representation. And judging from that scene back at the beach, I'd say she's right."

"Do you have any contraband on you?" Ryan asks Raymond.

"Excuse me?"

"Contraband, sir," Ryan repeats as he looks into the rearview mirror. "You know, like a candy bar, or chips, or sweets of any kind."

"No," Raymond says. "I do not."

"Hand me your *murse*," Ryan says.

Raymond looks puzzled. "Trust but verify," Ryan tells him with a shrug.

"Fine," Raymond says. "But it's not a murse. It's a messenger bag."

"Just hand it over," Ryan orders.

"Yeah," I add. "It's like the zoo. Don't feed the elephants. Or the hippos."

"That's not what I meant, Emery," Ryan backpedals. "I know you have willpower. It's just my job. Doc would kill me if—"

"It's fine, Ry," I interrupt. "I get it. And up until a few days ago, I totally would have been rifling through Raymond's bag for a Snickers."

Raymond leans forward and drops his black "messenger bag" into Ryan's lap as we pull into the driveway. Ryan parks the van and rifles through the bag. He pulls out an iPad, a wallet, a folder filled with papers, and several glossy celebrity trash-a-zines.

"And what is this?" Ryan asks, holding up a mushy Peppermint Pattie wrapper.

Ryan slouches. "I forgot, yeah, sorry. That thing has been in there for months."

Ryan hands Raymond back his murse. "My job is to protect Emery," Ryan explains. "Her biggest enemy isn't the paparazzi.

It's food." It's kind of sexy how Ryan is protecting me, but if he weren't so cute I would want to disembowel him for keeping me apart from a sweet.

"Understood," Raymond says, following us into the backyard, where Ryan disappears into the house and I promptly lie down in a patch of grass and soak in some morning rays before DD gets back and abuses me.

"Don't worry about Ryan," I tell Raymond. "Doc told him that if I gain any weight that he will fire his ass. He's kind of on edge."

"Fine," he says. "We all have our jobs. His is to protect you from yourself. Mine is to protect you from the media."

"I think I am doing just fine so far," I boast. "I'm getting skinnier every day and I have gotten famous pretty fast and all."

"Sure, you have," he says. "But this is just round one of a fifteen-round fight. There is a pattern with the media that will evolve as you play this fame game. I've seen it happen a million times before. The media loves you at first. The magazines throw you on their covers, build you up, blow smoke up your ass, pump up your image. They might seem like your friend, but then they proceed to tear you right down. If things aren't managed the right way, you can lose the game very quickly. I want to help you win."

"So why are you here?"

"Emery, you've got thirty-eight days before the final weigh-in. Right now, the media is in a honeymoon phase with you. They are infatuated." He hands me a tabloid magazine. "This just hit the newsstands."

The cover is a picture of me in my bikini, standing on the scale in my white bikini. I cringe at the sight of my hippo thighs.

The headline blares, **THE FIGHT OF HER LIFE: THE SECRET DISEASE THAT MIGHT STOP EMERY JACKSON FROM REALIZING HER MILLION-DOLLAR DREAM.**

"I have a disease?" I ask.

"I read the inside story," Raymond says. "Sources claim that due to your being lactose intolerant, you might have a genetic disorder preventing you from losing weight as fast as you will need to. They quote some expert about it."

"Well, I mean, I do get bloaty and farty. . . ."

"But it's all BS!" he counters. "Your gas issues aren't going to stop you from losing the weight. We are in the second week and they are already making up stories. That's exactly why Lana has me here. The tabloids will just make things up to sell magazines. That's why we need to keep putting our message out there. Perception is reality."

"So what's the plan?"

"For now, just keep doing what you're doing," he explains. "Keep dieting, exercising, losing the weight, doing what Team Fifty tells you to do. And very important: Keep making your video blogs. Those videos are really connecting with the audience. The research shows that you are getting more digital impressions than any other celebrity YouTube channel."

"Including Jenna Marbles?"

"Yes," he replies. "Including Jenna Marbles."

The fact that I am a bona fide YouTube star means more to me than the ten pounds I lost last week. It means more to me than the monster ratings on the show. My vlog is "connecting" with people.

I am not invisible. I do matter.

"Back to the media plan," Raymond continues. He is earnest, as if he cares. I get the impression he is around thirty—just old enough to have been around the block but not so old he has grown cynical about a job that isn't exactly about saving the world. "We will let the media keep reporting on you, keep running photos of you, covering your daily ups and downs and whatever else. The gossip websites and celebrity magazines will build you up, make you even more famous than you already are. This is all good. And when there are false stories out there—and there will be—we will feed different outlets stories that counteract the false ones. Of course, we will also activate your growing social media power to continue your dialogue with fans of the show. Then, leading up to the big finale, we will allow a few key journalists to interview you, to build up the hype and promote tune-in for the finale."

Raymond pulls out a few magazines from his murse.

"My boyfriend is a celebrity," he explains.

It's superficial of me, but now I like Raymond even more.

"He and his famous friends hate the magazines because they make up so much crazy stuff. So they have made up nicknames for the rag mags. *Us* magazine is 'Puss' magazine. *OK!* is 'Not OK!' *Life & Style* is 'Lies & Vile.' *In Touch* is 'Out of Touch.' What I'm trying to say is be prepared for some crazy stories. You best keep a sense of humor."

"Okay, so then what happens after that?" I ask.

He smiles. "Then you win your million dollars and Lana Sinclair promotes me. Everybody wins."

As I ponder just what I will do with my half of the prize, Angel storms into the backyard.

"I can't believe this is happening," she huffs. She collapses so hard into the patio chair her fake boobies almost pop out of her jogging bra, which the cameraman zooms in on. "This show is a total joke."

"What are you talking about?" I ask her.

"They made me take the bus back here all by myself," she whines. "The bus! I have never, ever taken the bus—ever. The bus, Emery! They made me take the freakin' hobo train."

#

Dr. Gen has done it. She finally wore me down. Her constant spot-on questions, her sympathetic gaze, her empathetic head nods, and that sensitive-sounding French accent. She finally broke me. Yes, Dr. Gen has made me cry.

"It's okay, Emery." She leans forward and hands me a Kleenex. "Let it all out. Sixteen years of pain. You deserve this moment."

Sixteen. The instant she utters the word it's as if my tear faucet went from half to full-on flow. And I can't stop it. They are a Niagara Falls of pent-up angst and sadness that has been building for a long time. For as long as I can remember. No matter how many times I sniffle and pinch shut my eyes. I've suddenly become one of them: emotional roadkill on the reality TV highway. And my pancake-flat corpse of shameless tears was triggered by one simple question: "Are you keeping a secret?"

The question triggers tears like those Big Mac billboards trigger hunger pangs.

The thing is, I just assumed everyone had things that they tucked in their brains, buried deep into their memory banks, draped underneath blankets of shame and remorse so thick that no one, not even yourself, can access. But Dr. Gen, this way-too-pretty psychotherapist sitting across from me, has opened up the box.

"What is your secret, Emery?"

I blow my nose, lest some snot ruin what surely will be TV gold. "If I told you, then it wouldn't be a secret," I joke.

Dr. Gen is laughing along with me.

"Everyone has secrets," she assures me. "Some are okay to keep. Others must be let out or they can grow toxic, eat away at you little by little." She uncrosses and then recrosses her skirted legs and leans in. "And some secrets can kill you."

I exhale. I realize that if I say it, I won't be able to take it back. I'm also fully aware that millions of people will also find out this something that I have been keeping under tight wraps for a good one year, two months, and seven days. But who's counting? Dr. Gen sits patiently, just as she has for every one of our daily sessions for nearly two weeks in the brain bunker, which is what I have taken to calling the basement den Doc has turned into Dr. Gen's office.

The silence between us is uncomfortable. There are a few things I am really not good at: good-byes, math, not eating at night, sports, and silence.

"I don't know," I say. "I wouldn't call it a secret, necessarily."

"Then what would you call it?"

"Just something I don't like to talk about."

"A lot of people might call that a secret," she reasons.

I can feel my shoulders, already sore from the barbell lifts yesterday, tightening up. I purse my lips and listen to her.

"When we are children, we are open books; we are so honest and truthful and free from secrets," she continues. "This is the healthiest, natural way to live. But along the way, we learn to hold back information. Maybe a friend tells you something and makes you swear you can't tell anyone, but when you mistakenly do, it causes such discomfort and pain that your body learns very quickly it doesn't feel good to reveal important secrets. The problem is that it also weighs a heavy burden on you to keep it inside, especially if it is something you have done, or seen, or been a part of in some way. What we fear most is not people finding out the secret, but the judgment and humiliation you might feel for revealing it. Your fear is understandable, but as your therapist, I am here to tell you that it is also psychologically taxing, not to mention in many cases physically debilitating. And this safe place is the place where you can share your secrets."

"Okay," I say. "I will think about it."

"Promise?"

"I promise." I hide my right hand beside my thigh and cross my fingers as a jinx. "Totally promise."

But what Dr. Gen doesn't seem to realize is that there are just some secrets too embarrassing to reveal. Ever.

III. ENTRÉE

SUNDAY, DECEMBER 15 (DAY 14)

I'm standing in front of the camera next to the scale. My Week Two live weigh-in is just minutes from now, and Raymond informs me that thanks to the episode that has just run for the last nearly two hours, Angel is already getting beat up in social media about her pity party over taking the bus back home from the beach.

In fact, #HoboTrain is trending on Twitter and Angel has the public approval rating of a Middle Eastern dictator.

"Cool," Angel reacts when Raymond tells us the #HoboTrain news.

Raymond whispers into my ear, "She has no clue how bad this makes her look."[9]

The stage manager alerts us that we have one minute.

Fifty . . . Fifty . . . Fifty . . . Fifty . . .

At first it is a muffled chant.

---

[9] Within minutes, the NAAHP (National Association for the Advocacy of Hobo People) has fired off a flurry of angry tweets and called for a boycott of the show.

Fifty . . . Fifty . . . Fifty . . . Fifty . . .

Then it builds to more than that.

"What's that noise?" I ask Doc.

"That's the sweet sound of success." Doc tells a crew member to pull open the living-room window curtains. "This is what happens when twenty million people start watching every episode. This is what happens when you become a YouTube star. You've gone viral, my love. Take a look for yourself. They're all here for you."

Fifty . . . Fifty . . . Fifty . . . Fifty!

A flurry of camera-phone flashes erupts the moment the curtain peels back. There have to be hundreds of people, the majority of them teenage girls, standing in the street in front of my house. Police have erected barricades on my front lawn to keep them at bay. I wonder if they mistakenly believe a boy band is holed up in my house. This is insane.

I study the crowd more closely and notice many of the girls have cut their hair short, into a shelfy bob. They are wearing "The Emery." *Holy crap.*

The curtains are shut, and as Doc welcomes back the audience, I tighten the belt of my robe, testing to see if it is more—or less—snug than it was for last week's successful weigh-in.

"Expect the unexpected," Doc tells the camera. "That's our motto here on *Fifty Pounds to Freedom*. And in keeping with our promise, we are going to switch things up a bit tonight. You might recall that last week we had all four members of Emery's inner circle reveal whether they thought Emery had lost the one pound a day she will need to average in order to reach her goal of fifty pounds in fifty days. Each of them revealed their prediction after

Emery weighed in. This week, however, we are going to have her mom, dad, sister, and boyfriend show us their prediction *before* she steps on the scale." Doc motions in the direction of the couch. "Another change: This time we are ditching the cards, and each of them will simply tell us whether they think Emery has lost seven pounds in the last seven days. Last week she wowed us all by going from 199 to 189 pounds in the first seven days."

He calls over Double D and Jackie. "As her trainer," he asks DD, "how do you explain last week's impressive performance?"

"Hard work, dedication, and balls of steel," he answers. "She shocked her body into action and we saw the results on the scale."

"And you, Jackie?"

"Emery has been dedicated to her diet, adhering strictly to her Freedom Menu™, and coupled with the calorie burn from her FreedomWorkout™, we saw results. I would expect nothing less."

I clasp my hands in front of myself as if in prayer, which I am, and I try to swallow my saliva. But there is none.

"Now remember," Doc adds. "Just like last week, for every wrong prediction by her inner circle, ten thousand dollars will be deducted from the family's one-million-dollar cash prize."

Then one by one, from left to right, Doc elicits a prediction from each.

Dad: "Just like last week, I have no doubt in my mind that Emery will be on course."

Mom: "Yes, she will. We believe in you, Em-Em!"

Angel: "Emery probably, I mean, yes definitely, has lost seven pounds."

Ben: "There is no stopping Emery. Yes."

"There you have it, America," Doc says. "Now, Emery, let's get to the moment we've all been waiting for."

He strolls back to me at the scale and faces the camera. "After the break."

MONDAY, DECEMBER 16 (DAY 15)

I knew it before I even stepped on that scale.

I knew it the second that I left therapy with Dr. Gen on Friday night, suffered a severe Big Mac attack, and sneaked off to McDonald's.

I knew it later, after therapy, when I went out back behind the garage to my candy stash and binged on Twix bars and candy corn.

I knew I would fail.

I knew I would disappoint.

I knew I would step on that scale and all the faith and support and love I felt in that room would evaporate.

So when the lights dimmed and the scale ticked up to 193.5 lbs and the roaring crowd fell silent, I knew what I felt like: the biggest loser.

I also knew the second I sat down on Dr. Gen's Couch of Truth some fifteen hours later that she would be grilling me about my epic fail.

"Is there anything you'd like to talk about?" she asks.

"As a matter of fact, yes." I squirm on my seat cushion, trying to get comfortable. But I can't. There is nothing comfortable about undergoing psychotherapy with the knowledge that everything you are saying is being documented for the entertainment of millions of people.

But now that I have indicated there is, in fact, something I want to say, I better come up with something fast.

"What is it?" Dr. Gen asks. "Do you want to talk about last night?"

"Sure."

"How did it make you feel?"

"Crappy, duh. I feel like I let a lot of people down."

"Don't worry about others, Emery. Worry about yourself."

"You're right. But I am worried about myself. I want to win. But maybe I just can't do it. Maybe I am physically unable to lose that much weight. Maybe I am just not wired for it. Maybe it is out of my control."

Dr. Gen flips open her laptop and turns it to face me. "Was doing this out of your control?"

She presses Play on a video that shows surveillance camera footage of me chowing down candy like a starving monkey would a pile of bananas.

Rather than embarrassed or betrayed or violated, I feel relieved.

"Yes, I cheated," I tell her. "You caught me. Guilty as charged. There, I'm a cheater."

"What do you feel when you see yourself in this video?"

"I feel human," I say. "I'm tired of hiding."

"Like the bank robber who is really hoping to get caught so she can stop the charade?"

"Yes," I reply. "Maybe. Something like that."

FRIDAY, DECEMBER 20 (DAY 19)

My day is all but done. Dinner was a very unsatisfying chicken breast with green beans and two glasses of water. And now I have an hour or so to get some homework done.

My phone rings. It's Ben.

"Emski! Let's go and kick it old school."

We both know what that means.

"Coffee Beach," we say in stereo.

Ben adds, "Two forks and two dorks."

Coffee Beach is where every teenager in Highland goes to hang out and do homework. We're too young to go to the bars, and "CB" is open until midnight. So when you also factor in the cozy couches, free Wi-Fi, and two-dollar bottomless cups of coffee, it's basically teen nirvana. CB is also where Ben and I met last year.

We were both in line to order, and when we stepped to the two registers at the same time, we ordered the same thing, the "CB Super Cinnamon Roll." A puffy confection of grease and sugar that remains my fave, though I can't currently eat such a treat. We both looked at each other and smiled, and Ben offered, "We can share."

And there we sat at the table by the front window. We may have been the two fattest kids at Highland, but becoming friends, then boyfriend-girlfriend, made me feel like I wasn't a freak for the first time.

The moment I step inside Coffee Beach (followed by a cameraman and Ryan), every head turns—including that of Ben, who's standing at the counter with the hugest smile. A few weeks ago, every kid in this place would have ignored me, or, at best, glanced up and then went back to their homework the second they saw my rotund self. In Highland, if you're fat, kids just assume you are lazy or somehow a flawed, sad person. So you avert your eyes.

Not now, though. Instead, my grand entrance sparks a wave of whispered conversation and stares. One girl points at me and I can see her mouthing *that girl Emery Jackson*. Another sneaks a pic off her camera phone, and I feign embarrassment. As Ryan quietly asks the dozen or so people inside to sign the production release form that allows the show to use them, I settle into our favorite window table while Ben orders a cinnamon roll.

The other kids continue to gawk at me, pretending to be doing their homework when, in fact, they are gossiping that The Emery Jackson has entered the coffee shop and they are so starstruck they could just wet themselves.

"One fork," I tell Ben as he puts the plate with the giant roll on the table. "Team Fifty will kill me if I even touch that."

Ben puts a bottle of water in front of me. Flipping open his laptop, Ben begins, "Okay, let's get this paper started."

I have been keeping up on our AP History classwork with my homeschool tutor provided to me by THE NETWORK, but having Ben in my class and as my partner on this essay assignment is even more of a bonus.

"Okay," Ben begins. "All we gotta do is compare and contrast the political philosophies of the founding fathers. Easy shmeasy."

"I have to say, I have trouble remembering all of them." I glance at the list. "Franklin, Jefferson, Washington. It's hard to tell them apart. They're all white and have Drunk Guy Face."

"What does that mean?"

"Their faces." I really do love jerking Ben's chain. "They are all red and they look bloated. I bet Ben Franklin was an alcoholic. I have always thought that."

"Shut up. That's ridiculous, Em. How do you know that?"

"Well, his nose was swollen. Always a sign. And he was quite chubby, had something of a beer belly if you ask me. And then there's that famous quote, from like Ben Franklin or somebody, that goes, 'Beer is proof that God loves us and wants us to be happy.' I can't believe you never heard that."

Ben is book smart, but sometimes he is just downright street stupid. Meanwhile, I am a repository of random quotes and facts and otherwise useless information.

"I am not kidding," I say. "Google it."

Ben stands up. "I'll tell ya what. I'm going to the bathroom. But I still don't believe Ben Franklin said that. Google it. If you're wrong, you buy me another cinnamon roll and I get to make out with you in front of all your little fans. If I'm wrong, I will streak down Sea Spray in your weigh-in bikini."

"Deal," I agree, rotating his laptop to face me as he walks off.

I open the browser and, being too lazy to type Google into the address line, I go to Bookmarks to find the homepage.

My jaw drops to the table when I see the list of websites on Ben's bookmarks:

Naked Teen Hotties

Skinny Chicks XXX

Down & Dirty Cheerleaders

College Girls Gone Crazy

Bikini Beach Babes

Petite and Horny Hos

The list of smut goes on and on. My heart feels as if it is going to pound through my chest. My face feels as if it's on fire. I want to hurl.

I click on the browser History bar, and lo and behold, there are hundreds—literally hundreds—of more addresses of disgusting porn websites that he has apparently been looking at and doing God knows what to. My stomach grinds tightly and I start feeling dizzy.

The cameraman sitting at a table points his hand-held cam at me, takes his eye off the lens, and asks, "Are you okay?" I must look like a corpse. I certainly feel like one.

Before I can answer, Ben returns and sits in his seat across from me. It's all I can do not to barf all over the table. It is as if I am looking at a different person. He is no longer the person I thought he was. Turns out, he's not different than the other guys who just want skinny girls with big boobs, little asses, and perfect little bodies. He is a dog. No, make that Dog, with a capital *D*.

"So what's the answer?"

I'm so dazed that I have no freakin' clue what he's talking about. "What?" I reply faintly. I'm staring blankly at the computer screen, an image of a girl with long blonde hair and a tattoo on her pelvis flashes in a pop-up screen.

"Our bet," he says. "Was Ben Franklin an alcoholic or not?"

"I don't know. But I hear that he was into porn."

"Huh?" Ben flashes a confused look. "Ben Franklin?"

I turn the laptop back around to face him and add, "Pervert."

His eyes pop open like giant saucers and he gulps a swallow of his own spit.

"Now I see why you're so busy on your laptop all the time." I push his cinnamon roll off his plate and onto his lap and everyone in the coffee shop turns and stares. "You're a disgusting pig, just like every other guy."

I notice everyone is still staring at me as if I am a crazy hobo. I take to my feet and announce, "Take a picture, it will last longer. And if it's a nude picture, give it to this guy." I point at Ben. "He loves porn."

"Emery," he hushes me. "Sit down. Let's talk about this. Why are you surfing porn on my computer?" Ben grabs the roll that has since fallen to the floor and places it on the table. He lowers his voice to a whisper. "I have no idea how that got on there."

"Yeah, right. Don't lie to me."

"Wait," he says. "So you think I am surfing all this porn?"

"It's your computer, isn't it? I mean, SkinnyBitches.com? Really, Ben? I mean, seriously? Is this what you want me to look like? Is this why you're being so supportive of me losing weight, so I can become some fantasy porn queen?"

"Look, Emery, I don't know how all this got on here. I would never surf these kinds of—"

"Dude. Just stop. The least you could have done is delete the History. I mean, if you're going to be a sick perv looking at naked girls you could at least clear your browser."

"First of all," he says. "I swear I wasn't browsing those sites."

"And second of all, none of them look like your fat girlfriend." I laugh manically. "You probably want these girls. Go get them, I don't care. I'm done with fake people. I'm done with people pretending to be one thing but really being another."

"Emery, listen to me."

"Talk is cheap. You're probably a sex addict. Is that why you tell me how beautiful I am? Just to butter me up to use me and think of some other skinny girl? And I thought you were different."

There's nothing he can say to stop my wave of anger, hurt, and embarrassment—all being caught on camera. Somewhere, probably out in the production van watching the live feed from the camera, Doc is watching this melodrama with glee.

"I thought that you loved me no matter how big I am. Wow, I am such an idiot for falling for that line."

"Em, you're not an idiot at all. Stop it." He slams closed the laptop. "Listen to me. It's not what it looks like."

"And neither are you."

Ben sits lifelessly in his chair, shoulders slouched forward. He keeps shaking his head. Tiny beads of sweat are bubbling on his forehead.

"I think you should leave," I say. "Just get your fat ass out of here. Like now. Before I kill you."

When Ben refuses to get up, Ryan steps forward. He slides his headset off, hitches it to his belt, and lets it dangle sexily.

"Everything okay here?" Ryan asks me, his eyes darting over at Ben.

"No," I reply. "Make him leave."

Ryan grabs Ben by the back of his arm. "Hey, buddy," Ryan says. "You should go. Really, you should. Like now."

SATURDAY, DECEMBER 21 (DAY 20)

Jackie is already waiting in the kitchen when I shuffle down at around six thirty for breakfast.

"Morning, sunshine," my peppy nutritionist chirps all chipper-like.

I grumble words that are of no known language. Not a morning person, especially after I cried myself to sleep at around three in the morning.

"Have a seat, Emery," Jackie says, pointing at a sad, little meal she has laid out on the counter.

"You okay?" she asks.

"Define okay."

"You look like you didn't sleep. Those bags under your eyes. Maybe you need more protein."

"No, I just need a new boyfriend."

"What about Ben?"

"We broke up last night."

"Why? I thought you guys were so in love."

"Yeah, we were. Until I found out he was cheating on me with his computer."

"What are you talking about?" Jackie pours a powdered vitamin C packet into my water. "How can someone cheat with a computer? You mean, like he was talking to girls on the Internet?"

"No, just surfing porn. But I'd rather not talk about it," I say. "I'd rather focus on winning this stupid show. And not being a fat pig."

Jackie offers me a pity face and sits on the stool beside me. "Oh, Emery, you're not a fat pig. You're a work-in-progress. You have been doing great. Negative self-talk won't make you skinny. Stay positive and positive change will happen. In life, you get what you give."

"What happens when you just want to give up?"

"You don't," she says. "I don't know if I ever told you, but the whole reason I got into exercise and nutrition is because I wasn't too different from you. You know how in college they talk about 'The Freshman Fifteen'? Well, I packed on thirty pounds my first year of college. Thirty! Then one day, I looked in the mirror while drying off after a shower and saw my naked body and I broke down and started to cry. Just lost it. Look at me now: I'm a size two, super famous, and my body fat is under five percent. That makes me a triple threat. And you want to be a triple threat, right? Don't you, Emery?"

"Uh, I guess so," I say. "But I don't really want to be famous. Honestly, I'd rather not be famous."

"Well, I hate to break it to you, but everyone who is famous eventually becomes skinny."

"But Lena Dunham isn't skinny."

"Oh, don't worry, she probably will be someday. Like physics, the world of celebrity has its own laws. And that is one of them: an object that tends to be fat doesn't stay fat for long."

"Jackie," I say, "I honestly couldn't give two craps about Lena Dunham. I just don't want to be invisible anymore. I want guys to be attracted to me. For once, I want to be a sex object. I want to be wanted. I want to be lusted after. So, yes, I want to do this. Yes, I do."

"So are you saying you want to be skinny?"

"Yes, fine, I want to be skinny. But shouldn't I be healthy?"

Jackie places her hands on each of my shoulders and looks me in the eye. "Honey, when I am done with you, you will be healthy. And skinny."

I'm not sure what to make of her promise. From everything I have always read, it is more important to be healthy than to be skinny—no matter what the media images tell us. But Jackie, if anything, is one very persuasive FFG[10]. "Okay, let's do it," I say. "I'm all in."

"That's great!" Jackie bounces on her Nikes. "This is the first time you have actually said it! And to say it is to believe it. And to believe it is to *achieve* it! And it's a good thing because your weigh-in is tomorrow, and, well, last week didn't go very well. To get on schedule for the fifty pounds in fifty days and get to twenty-one pounds lost, you will have to lose fourteen pounds this week. According to my calculations, this is not at all possible on the current program, even with all the exercise you've been doing. So we are going to change things up a little bit in the diet department. And when I am done with you after these fifty

---

[10] Former Fat Girl.

days, Ben is going to be looking at sexy photos of YOU."

"Lucky me." I sigh.

"Here's the new breakfast for the New-and-Improved Emery™," Jackie says.

I look down at half of a whole-grain English muffin, one egg white, and a few slices of apple. "Seriously?"

"A hundred and ten calories," she says. "We are taking you to the next level. We need to get you to under 800, all while keeping a balanced diet. It's simply time for more drastic measures."

Mom walks in. "Yummy, yummy, yummy!" she enthuses. "Is this the new diet plan?"

I have already started eating the "meal" as I notice Mom giving me the once-over. I can tell she is looking at my butt stuffed into the black stretch workout pants and thinking maybe my 110-calorie breakfast is too much. Her poisoned facial expression says it all. It always has. It is the same glance she gives Angel. The one that says, "I am inspecting your body to make sure you don't look any fatter because if you are then I take that as a personal reflection of my failure as a parent."

"This is what we have you eating from now on." Jackie drops a piece of paper next to my plate. Mom looks over my shoulder as I read it.

> Breakfast: Half whole-grain English muffin with egg white and apple slices (110 calories)
>
> Late a.m. snack: Half a cup of berries (60 calories)
>
> Lunch: 8 ounces of turkey (240 calories), PLUS: FreedomShake™ (80 calories)

Afternoon snack: 4 almonds, 2 celery sticks (50 calories)

Dinner: 112 grams of baked whitefish, steamed broccoli, and asparagus (250 calories)

"Isn't this a little extreme?" I ask.

Jackie shrugs her shoulders. "Doc is worried," she answers. "He's afraid you won't even be close and the fans will be turned off. This is what he wants."

"And what's this FreedomShake™?" I ask.

"It's a soy drink packed with some vitamins and supplements that will jump-start your metabolism."

Mom puts her arm around me and bends over. She kisses me on the cheek. "I am so proud of you, Emmy," she coos. "We believe in you. You will win this war."

War is right. A war against myself. A war against the skinny naked chicks on Ben's computer. A war against the entire looks-obsessed world.

I have spent the last three days crying . . . starving myself . . . crying . . . starving myself some more . . . working out like a fiend with DD . . . and all the while ignoring the constant texts from Ben insisting that the porn on his laptop wasn't his.

> Em, I don't surf that garbage . . . u gotta believe
> me . . . I miss my dork . . . you are beautiful . . .
> honestly, some1 hacked me . . .

And in between all this drama I've been sitting on Dr. Gen's couch trying to make sense out of the disaster that has become my life. I can't remember the last time I laughed or made some-one laugh. It used to be my M.O. But Dr. Gen thinks I have always used humor as a self-defense, as a shield against criticism or people's judgment of me for being a Big Girl. She thinks it is a good sign that instead of just brushing off everything with self-deprecating fat jokes, I am letting myself feel.

Right this second, however, I feel sore. And tired. And hungry. But more than anything, I feel afraid. I'm afraid to fail. I'm afraid to be alone. I'm afraid I will let everyone down. I'm afraid that my secret will come out.

SUNDAY, DECEMBER 22 (DAY 21)

I peek through the curtain in my bedroom window. Down below, the crowd is gathered. There must be like a thousand—literally a *thousand*—people huddled in the street, the swelling masses being the reason why some of the cops are dressed in riot gear. A few cops even sit on horseback. There are also more people holding signs than last week. A lot more.

YOU CAN DO IT, EMERY!

JUST SAY NO TO FAT!!!

Young and old, these fans have come to be closer to the weigh-in. I notice that most have one thing in common. Most are overweight. It's as if I am their messiah of moose-hood. As if by being close to me losing weight they somehow will be able to as well. And as if this isn't all getting stalker-ish enough, more of them are wearing "The Emery" hairdo. I have created a monster.

And THE NETWORK is feeding it. I spot a team of "Freedom Fighters" in red, white, and blue tracksuits handing out free samples of FreedomShakes™ and samples from the Freedom Menu™.

It's not as if they can see anything special. But there's something about a TV camera—especially a live TV camera—that makes people do silly things. They say there's a price of fame, that it can destroy lives and turn otherwise normal people into raging egomaniacs with drug addictions. So far, though, fame has been pretty darn good to me.

Besides a few weirdos in my YouTube comments telling me they want to tie me up naked and feed me onion rings (we alerted the FBI), the whole celebrity thing has been pretty cool. All the mean girls from Highland now want to be my friend and kiss my ass. Everyone—from Ellen to Barbara Walters to Oprah—calls Raymond every day requesting the first interview with me after the show ends. All kinds of companies send me free stuff—shoes, pants, shorts, phones, shirts, makeup, books, magazines, perfume, health food, bikinis, tampons, you name it. As for the paparazzi, they're nice for the most part. The best advice Raymond has given me is to make sure to always smile. That way, the paps can't sell a picture claiming I'm angry or upset about something, which, he says, is more valuable. Happy doesn't sell, but drama does.

Speaking of drama, tonight has plenty of it. Even though I can't imagine eating less or working out any more, I fear that I haven't lost any weight. I fear that all this hard work and sacrifice is a giant waste of time. Maybe my body just isn't meant to be thin. Maybe being fat is simply a death sentence that I have to accept.

As usual before every weigh-in, Ryan knocks on my bedroom door. I tighten the belt of my robe and open it.

"I bet you wish I wasn't wearing anything," I crack. "I mean, I am so sexy and all."

Ryan giggles. "I wish a lot of things," he says. "One being that you won't give me a heart attack and will come with me right now for the weigh-in—before Doc kills me!"

He adds, "Before we go downstairs, I just want to say I'm really sorry about what went down with Ben and all."

"I guess we provide a valuable public service to guys everywhere."

"And what would that be?"

"To delete the History."

We share a laugh for a moment, but he glances at his watch.

"Don't worry, we will head down," I tell him. "But before we go downstairs, can I ask you something?"

"Yes, but make it fast. Seriously, Doc is yelling in my headset as we speak."

"Be honest." I open my robe and flash Ryan a look at my bikini-clad body. "How do I look? Do you think I lost any weight this week?"

Ryan nervously looks at my body with his deep-set green eyes, which work their way up to my eyes.

"You look amazing," he says. "You always have. To me."

"I don't feel amazing. I feel grosser than ever. I feel fat. I feel unattractive. I feel deathly afraid of standing on that scale again until I am not fat. I am scared, Ryan."

Ryan exhales and looks around the room nervously. "I know it's scary. I feel for you."

He steps closer to me and leans in with a whisper. "Just be careful. Things aren't what they seem."

I tilt my head, confused. Ryan makes the "shush" sign with his forefinger in front of his gorgeous lips. He adds softly, "Just be careful."

Even though I'm totally unsure what he's talking about, I nod in agreement anyway.

Ryan presses his headset against his right ear. "Seriously, now they are insisting we get down there. We go live in two minutes."

I follow Ryan down the stairs, noticing how his jeans contour around his butt in a way that mine never will. I may no longer have a boyfriend, but I decide I do have a crush. Or at least a very cute distraction.

"It has been quite the week for Emery Jackson," Doc opens the show with his usual flair. "Her week started with the reality that after losing an impressive ten pounds in her first week, she had shockingly gained four and a half pounds in her second week. On top of that, her family's grand prize was shrunk to $950,000 after the first weigh in—after her sister Angel wrongly predicted Emery would not meet her goal. And if this weren't disappointing enough, Emery suffered a painful breakup with her boyfriend, Ben, as you just saw on tonight's episode."

"But Emery, she is a fighter. She has the spirit of a warrior. I think all of you will agree that there is something special about Emery Jackson. With the help of Team Fifty, she picked herself up by her bootstraps and has rededicated herself to meeting her goal of losing fifty pounds in fifty days. But tonight, on this Day Twenty-One, we are going to do something different from past weigh-ins. Gone will be the predictions from her family. Tonight we are putting Emery in control of her own destiny. Tonight Emery will decide whether she wants to get on the scale."

This definitely is news to me.

Doc smiles and continues. "For those among you twenty million viewers watching this live who aren't aware, we have banned Emery from weighing herself outside of these weekly, live weigh-ins. Weight loss is as much a mystery as it is a science. It is, at its heart, a body at war with itself. Is Emery winning her war against her weight? That is the question we may—or may not—get an answer to . . . after the break."

I've been standing off camera as Doc read his prompter like he was MLK delivering the "I Have a Dream" speech.

"What's happening?" I ask. "I thought I was just weighing in like every week."

Doc offers up a sly wink. "To make a good reality TV show, Emery, you can't ever let the audience or the participants get too comfortable. So we are shaking things up a little."

"And we're back," Doc announces moments later. "Day Twenty-One of *Fifty Pounds to Freedom*. Emery is almost halfway through her journey. Joining us now is the star, our doyenne of dieting, Emery Jackson. Come on out, young lady!"

I step out in my robe and slippers, and Doc drapes his arm over my shoulders. "Emery, it has been a tough week, hasn't it?"

"I guess you could say that."

"I know, dear. We all feel for you. And because it has been so demanding, so emotionally and physically draining, we are going to offer you an option tonight. Doing the math, you would have to weigh in at one hundred seventy-eight pounds in order to be on your pound-a-day pace. That would mean a total of fifteen and a half pounds lost in just seven days. We have talked to the experts and they tell us that, while possible, it is highly unlikely that you could have lost that much weight so fast. However—and I do add a major however here—your Team Fifty tells me that you have been a model client this week, that you have stuck to your Freedom Menu™, that you have done all your FreedomWorkouts™, and by the looks of things, your body is looking trimmer than ever. Indeed, you are becoming the New-and-Improved Emery™. But, of course, you never know until you step on the scale just how much progress you have made. So, Emery, tonight you will have the choice: You can step on the scale, and if you are back on your pound-a-day schedule and weigh one hundred seventy-eight pounds or less, we will reward you with—get ready for it—an extra $100,000."

Doc turns serious. "But if you weigh more than one hundred seventy-eight, Emery, it will cost you $100,000. The second option is for you to skip the scale right now and get on it next week. If you are one hundred seventy-one pounds or less, meaning back on schedule, you will not have lost any money."

I gulp nervously.

"So what will it be, Emery? Will you be stepping on the scale tonight?"

My mind is racing as fast as my heart is beating. Ryan did say I looked—what was it?—amazing. I have been working out like a mad woman. I did cut back on my calories and did not cheat at all. But did I drop from 193.5 pounds to 178 in just seven days?

"We need an answer," Doc presses. "So what will it be?"

I look across the room at Mom, Dad, and Angel, who is shaking her head no. Mom's face is, as usual, Botox-stiff, while Dad sits like an emotionless statue.

Suddenly I have an idea.

"I don't like my choices," I declare.

An idea that makes me feel a little bit—make that a lot—better about this weight-loss challenge fiasco.

Doc steps back. "Sorry, my dear, but you only have those two. You either step on the scale or you don't."

"I like a good challenge. So I would like a third option."

"Okay," Doc says with hesitation. "What is that?"

I notice beads of sweat forming on Doc's forehead. Clearly, he didn't expect me to throw him a curveball on live television.

"What if I don't step on a scale again until Day Fifty? I mean, to be honest, these weekly weigh-ins are very stressful. And I would rather just focus on my effort and not just the outcome. My very talented Team Fifty tells me this is the healthiest way to go about losing weight, actually. And like you've always said, this is about being healthy."

Doc's eyes dart around the room. The crew is standing there with blank stares, waiting for their master to react.

"I'll tell ya what," Doc says. "I will give you an answer to your question. After the break."

When we cut to commercial, Doc drops his hand down as if his mic is made of lead.

"What the hell are you doing? That was *not* in the script."

"But I thought our show was *unscripted*?"

"Yeah, just like there is a real Santa Claus," he snaps. "You can't just throw things out there like that on live television."

"I just thought it was only fair that I be given a healthy option." I smile wide. "You do want me to be a good role model for all those girls out there, don't you?"

"Yes, uh, of course," Doc stammers. "But a big decision like this is beyond my power. I have to call Lana. It will be her call. This will be a NETWORK decision. I'm just the producer."

"How much time we got, Tommy?" Doc asks the stage manager.

"Three and a half minutes," he answers.

Doc starts dialing Lana and walks out of the living room and into the basement. A couple minutes later, he returns with a smug look on his face, ignoring me. Obviously some sort of decision has been made.

"My gosh, talk about cliffhangers, America!" he announces when we return from break. "Emery has made a request. Instead of doing four more weigh-ins between now and Day Fifty, she would like to do just one on the very last day of our show. If she has lost the fifty, she gets her one million dollars. She thinks this is the healthy thing to do. Well, I have talked to the powers-that-be, and they agree with Emery. We will allow her to do this. So that she can focus on her exercise and nutrition and therapy. This is, after all, not just another reality show. We aren't doing all this for your entertainment and pleasure. This is not some sort of exploitative program. We have a heart. This show is about Emery finding true freedom."

Doc drapes his arm around me in that creepy way that he does.

"But, Emery, there is a catch," he says. "If you fail to lose the fifty pounds, we need you to agree ahead of time, here tonight in front of all of America, to one simple thing."

"Okay . . ."

"That if you fail to lose fifty pounds in fifty days, you will commit to returning for a second season, in which you will once again try to achieve the same goal of fifty in fifty."

The fear of having to stand in a bikini, exposing my blob of a body in front of millions, outweighs any fear I have of not losing the pounds—or any nausea I feel just thinking about having to go through another season.

I grab Doc's hand and squeeze it firmly. "Deal."

WEDNESDAY, DECEMBER 25 (DAY 24)

"Merry Christmas, Emery," Raymond says dejectedly. "Merry F'in Christmas!"

My normally jolly publicist tosses the magazine onto the ground between my spread-out legs. Not exactly the Christmas present I expected to get from him.

Stretching after my morning treadmill run, and perma-dizzy from cutting my daily calories nearly in half since Sunday's weigh-in debacle, I stare at the cover in a daze. I can barely bring the words into focus.

The headline screams in giant black lettering: EXCLUSIVE: EMERY'S SEX SECRETS REVEALED!!!

My first thought: Three exclamation points aren't really necessary.

"Is this true?" Raymond asks.

"Is what true?"

"The story," he responds. "That you have a sex secret! As

your publicist, I need to know. I'm getting a million emails from other media asking about it. Dr. Oz and Dr. Phil both already called."

"I don't know. What's it say exactly?"

"Just read it."

I flip open the rag mag and thumb through it. I find the cover story. Luckily, Josh was bluffing that night at the party when he threatened he had photos. Unfortunately, the text is damning enough.

> Reality star and weight-loss icon Emery Jackson has been keeping a secret. A real big secret.
>
> Sources exclusively tell *TV Weekly* that Emery engaged in a wild, drunken sex romp with two members of the Highland High School football team at a party last year. Emery was just fifteen at the time of the incident.
>
> "Emery and some other kids were playing 'Truth or Dare' and doing vodka shots all night," says a source with knowledge of the sex scandal. "One of the guys, a senior linebacker who was hosting the party at his house, dared her to have sex with him in his bedroom. Let's just say she accepted the dare." (*TV Weekly* is withholding the name of the boys because they are minors and, unlike Emery Jackson, are not public figures.)
>
> Another source tells *TV Weekly* that Emery returned to the party a half hour later and when another football player dared her to do it with him as well, she agreed. "Emery was very needy. She obviously had self-esteem issues and was desperate for attention," says the Highland insider. "The only reason this secret didn't get out was that the two

players were embarrassed that they had sex with her. She lost her virginity that night. It is just so sad." Adds the source, "When word got out that she was doing *Fifty Pounds to Freedom*, the boys started gossiping about it. Now everyone calls her 'Easy Emery' behind her back."

A fellow Highland High student tells *TV Weekly* that Emery's reputation is permanently stained. "Emery means well, but most of the girls have totally lost respect for her," says junior Kendra Harrison. "But we are praying for her."

An investigation by *TV Weekly* has also revealed that Emery has not yet told her ex-boyfriend, Ben, about her raunchy past. Speculation is that this wild night of risky sex is, in fact, the "secret" that Emery hinted at but failed to reveal while in therapy on a recent episode of her hit series.

Reba Myers, a world-renowned expert in teen sexuality, tells *TV Weekly* that it's not uncommon for obese teens to engage in promiscuous sexual behavior. "Recent studies do suggest that adolescents who are overweight are more likely to engage in risky sexual behavior than peers of normal weight," Myers says. "The reasons for this can range from depression, to the need to feel loved, to a low self-esteem that drives them to feel accepted. Girls who are obese often feel powerless, especially when it comes to competing with other girls for male attention. Having risky sex with multiple sex partners is unfortunately something that the obese girl thinks—consciously or not—will give her power. And when you add alcohol into the mix, it can lead to some very extreme behavior. She's just lucky she didn't get pregnant."

When I finish reading, I hand the magazine back to Raymond. I can barely breathe without that queasy feeling I get right before I am about to hurl. My life is over. I feel dead to the world.

Raymond kneels beside me on the grass.

"Seriously, Emery," he says. "THE NETWORK needs to know. Is this true? We need to issue some sort of statement."

"Tell them, 'no comment,'" I say.

"In this world, 'no comment' is the same as confirming it is true."

I stand up. "Just say, 'no comment,'" I repeat, then stomp into the house and down to the basement to find Dr. Gen. Our daily (entirely videotaped) appointment is set to start in ten minutes.

When I step inside the room, she's reading a copy of *TV Weekly*.

"Doing your research?" I ask her.

"Oh, Emery." Dr. Gen leaves the magazine on her desk and approaches me slowly. She takes off her glasses and wraps her petite arms around me. "I'm so sorry, Emery. I am so, so sorry."

Her hug doesn't squeeze the tears out of me like a wet sponge. I am too numb to cry.

"I take it this was your secret?" Dr. Gen says.

I nod yes.

"How does it make you feel?"

"Like this is a pretty crappy way to spend Christmas."

I pick up a pillow and throw it across the room. It sails into a bronze candle holder resting on a table, which topples into a decorative glass bowl, which shatters into hundreds of pieces when it hits the tile floor below.

I turn and stare into the camera that is fixed into the wall behind Dr. Gen's desk. "You got your money shot, Doc. Enjoy it, you sick bastard."

"You're angry," Dr. Gen says.

"Of course I am angry! I didn't decide to go on this show so that my deepest, darkest secrets could be exposed for all the world's entertainment. I came on this show to win a million dollars."

"And to lose weight."

"I guess so, yeah. But mostly to win a million dollars."

"Maybe there is some positive to come out of this, Emery. Maybe there is a therapeutic benefit to—"

"To public humiliation?" I interrupt.

"No, but a benefit to the secret being out there. Look, in life we don't get to choose what happens to us, but we do get to choose how we react to things. That is what really defines a person."

"Thanks for the pep talk, Coach," I grumble.

"I'm serious," she says. "Now that your secret is no longer a secret, we can talk about it."

"What's there to say? That the world just thinks I am a ho-bag who slept with a gazillion guys on a dare? What could I possibly learn from that?"

"You could learn perhaps why you did that, what motivated you to do something so extreme."

"I wanted to feel loved," I say. "I wanted to feel wanted. So I did it."

"But how did it really make you feel?"

"Used," I say. "I felt used."

"So you're just a victim in all this?"

"Kind of."

"Well, I would disagree," she challenges. "Yes, you are, in part, a victim. But I also believe you were a willing participant. Those boys didn't force you to have sex with them, did they?"

"No."

"Well, that's one good thing about this situation. You are very lucky. Date rape is, tragically, a lot more common than people think. But in your case, if you just paint yourself as a victim, then you are missing out on an opportunity to learn from what clearly you believe was a mistake.

"The first step to healing is to accept your role in what you did. If you don't accept your responsibility, then you are letting yourself off the hook too easily. I could sit here and tell you, 'Oh, poor Emery. Those boys preyed on your low self-esteem and need for acceptance and took advantage of you and now that you are famous someone is spreading the news of this mistake to the world. Poor, poor Emery.' But that would only be part of the story. You see, Emery, it is the story we tell ourselves that is our truth."

Dr. Gen gets up and sits next to me on the couch. She places her hand on my knee. "You can learn how to stop letting other people tell your story. What is your story, Emery?"

I stare down at the floor, thinking, for several seconds. I respond with the first thing that comes to mind.

"Revenge," I blurt out.

"Revenge?"

"Yes, revenge."

"Against whom?"

"Everyone."

"I don't believe you." Dr. Gen crosses her arms. "I think you were acting out against one person in particular."

"God?" I ask.

"He's not a person," Gen volleys back, rather impressively. "But I'm thinking of someone who is a person. Someone who I think has been a source of anger for you. Someone who you wish gave you more attention."

Dr. Gen and I lock eyes. We both know that I know the answer.

"Dad," I confirm.

"Let me ask you a question," she says. "Where is your dad right now?"

"I have no idea."

"Exactly. He is, essentially, MIA. In fact, even when he was signed on to appear on this show with you, he still managed to not be a part of your life. Even for the cameras, for the most part. Sounds to me like an absentee father."

"With all due respect, Doc, it doesn't take a genius to see that."

"You know what I think, Emery? I think you're not as much hungry for food as you are for a father. You are father hungry."

I take a deep breath and let it out and let her statement sink in. I'm smart enough to know where she is going with this, so I cut her off at the proverbial psychobabble pass.

"So you're saying that I went and had random sex with those guys because in my twisted subconscious, I was crying out for attention from my dad."

"That's a pretty mature conclusion to make," Dr. Gen says with a comforting smile. "But the question isn't what I think. It is whether you believe this to be true. Do you?"

Then I start crying. Like a baby.

DAY 26 VIDEO BLOG
SLUT-SHAMING AND OTHER HORRIBLE THINGS GIRLS DO TO OTHER GIRLS

Unless you are living under a rock, you've probably already heard the big, bad breaking news. You know, the news that that I am The World's Biggest Slut.

Go ahead. Google "world's biggest slut" and you will find no less than 23,456 results linking this phrase to my name. And by the time I am done ranting into this laptop cam like a lunatic it will probably be over 24,334.

This whole assault on my character is a perfect example of a phenomenon that is called "slut-shaming." If you aren't familiar with the term, don't worry. I looked it up and here's the definition: "The act of making someone, usually a woman, feel guilty or inferior, for engaging in certain sexual behaviors that violate traditional gender expectations." I am used to being the victim of "fat-shaming," which, by just slotting out a few words, can be defined as "the act of making someone, usually a woman, feel guilty or inferior, for looking bigger to the point that it violates traditional gender expectations."

When you've spent most of your life looking like I do, you learn that people can be very judgmental and lame. Sad, but true. But honestly, I am not going to sit here in my bedroom—which, by the way, all you haters, I have had sex in with my boyfriend!—and even bother refuting people who call me a slut. Or fat. It's just not worth my time.

What I really want to talk about is why do girls feel so obligated to put down and judge other girls so much? I have heard girls attack other girls for being too pretty, too ugly, too pale, too tan, too tall, too short, having small boobs, having big boobs, and being too friendly or too shy. Admit it: everyone watching this video has been judged for being one of these "toos."

Each and every one of us is here on this Earth because two people decided to do the dirty deed. Hate to break it to you innocents, but there is no stork appearing out of the blue sky and delivering babies from heaven. Ear muffs on all the little kiddies out there: we are all here because of sex!

So on one level, I would argue that to be Pro Sex is to be Pro Life. Obviously, I don't want to upset a whole other group of people, but I am trying to make this very valid and relevant (to every human being) point: Sex is overwhelmingly a positive thing. It is what we are, biologically speaking, wired to do in order to keep the species alive. But we are not wild animals, and for that reason, I firmly believe (and not just because the Bible told me so) that we all shouldn't go around humping indiscriminately like a pack of wild rabbits just so that we can procreate.

We have souls.

This kind of reckless sexual behavior would not be a good thing, even if it felt good for some reason in the short run. There are diseases, there are feelings and emotions, and there are physical boundaries that everyone should erect around themselves if they indeed have enough self-respect to deem their body a temple. Especially if you are a young person and figuring your life out. Especially if you aren't in a committed relationship with someone who really loves you as a person and not some pleasure object. Especially if you aren't protected with the right stuff. Especially if you are doing it for the wrong psychological reasons, such as, well, to get boys to actually treat you like you are not invisible.

This, my Web friends, is exactly what I did.

Yes, the *TV Weekly* story is true. I did have a drunken night of sex and lost my virginity to two morons in a moment of very weak judgment and inebriation like a year ago. If I could do it all over again, I would not have been playing a stupid game of Truth or Dare with a bunch of Neanderthals. If I could do it all over again, I would have stopped and realized that what I needed wasn't sex, but to learn to love myself by not trying to get the approval of someone else.

I could lie to you all and say I only did it because I was drunk. Yes, a lot of kids my age love to use that excuse. But that would be a total cop-out. The truth is that what motivated me more than the vodka was the empty void that has been growing inside of me for as long as I can remember.

So, all you haters out there who have been spamming my Twitter, you can call me a slut all you want. Maybe this makes you feel better because it allows you not to focus on your own faults or your own choices. Maybe you have learned from society, perhaps subconsciously, that girls who have sex are bad and in order to keep the paternalistic order, we need to denigrate them as a way of keeping other girls from dangerously doing the same. But there is a whole other way to treat girls like me. It is to show compassion. It is to not judge, but rather to listen and learn and love.

As I sit here, exhausted physically from all this working out, I am also exhausted mentally. By having my dirty laundry aired—my secret exposed—I have been attacked by millions. It really sucks.

One of my favorite quotes of all time is, "To err is human; to forgive, divine." Well, even though I just spent a few minutes ranting about all of you haters, I forgive you. Now I just hope that, Ben, you can find it in your heart to do the same.

MONDAY, DECEMBER 30
(DAY 29)

"I don't do cheer anymore. You know that."

I am digging in my heels. Well, I am wearing running shoes, but you get the point.

"You can do it, honey," Mom insists. "You used to do cheer all the time when you were little. You must remember at least some of the moves."

"Yes, I do remember," I shoot back. "Which is exactly why I don't want to do this."

We are standing in the middle of the West Coast Supreme gymnastics studio for my late afternoon workout. Normally, DD has me do a sixty-minute circuit of weights, cardio, and stretching at the home gym, but when Mom overheard him suggest we do a "cross-training" activity on alternate days, she offered the brilliant idea doing cheer practice with Angel and her coach. Brilliant maybe for THE NETWORK, which has struck yet another branding deal with a line of cheerleader workout videos. For me, it is just a revisiting of my worst childhood nightmares of trying to keep up with Angel.

Angel may not be the only cheerleader at Highland, but she is the only one who is a member of the California state runner-up cheer team "West Coast Supreme."

I always hated cheer classes. First of all, tumbling makes me so dizzy I want to barf. Second of all, by the time I was nine, it became abundantly obvious to everyone that there was not a single cheerleader uniform that looked cute on my chunky little body. That's when I quit. Just like I quit volleyball, basketball, tennis, swimming, and soccer.

As I stand on this giant blue mat in my sweats I realize I haven't done gymnastics in eight years. The head coach of West Coast Supreme is the instructor, a hyperenergetic Aly Raisman lookalike in a pleated cheerleader skirt and top. She is twenty-four years old but looks eleven and speaks like she is nine.

As she bounces in front of us and the camera crew, it becomes obvious why I have been gone so long. But my judgment lapse is irreversible at this point and I'm stuck doing this.

"Hi, hi, Emery!" the instructor shouts with pep.

"Rah, rah, rah," I reply, shaking invisible pom-poms.

"I'm Kirby Jones." She claps three times. "Nice to meet you. You ready to get your CheerFreedom™ [11] on?"

She hoppity-hops over to her Angel and they high-five. "I know that *you* are ready," Kirby says. "Right, Angel Foodcake!"

The toxic twins high-five again and Kirby adds with way too

---

[11] The CheerFreedom™ DVD is available for "just $49.99" to subscribers of THE NETWORK YouTube channel. It comes with a set of pom-poms that you can use "in the comfort of your own home."

much enthusiasm for someone not on drugs, "Not only are you going to have an amazing workout, but you are going to have an amazing amount of fun, fun, fun!" Kirby is playing to the camera and barely even looking at me.

"Now, to warm up, we are going to start with some squats!" she announces.

Squats aren't among my favorite exercises. Not only do they remind me of peeing in the woods (which is gross), but they also make my knees creak.

"All righty," Kirby chirps after twenty down-and-ups. "Very good, girls. Today we are going to mostly focus on the abs and core. When is the last time you saw a top-level, elite cheerleader who didn't have abs of steel? That's right. You have never seen one. Why? Because a great, great, great cheerleader has great, great, great abs." Kirby seems almost OCD in her having to bark everything in threes. "And it starts with a strong core. I am going to show you five exercises to make you *abs*-olutely rock, rock, rock hard."

Kirby gets onto her stomach. Angel and I copy her.

"We're going to start with a plank," she says. "Make sure your body is flat like a board, arms at ninety degrees and shoulders back. And hold it for ten seconds."

I hold the position, with only my toes and bottom of my forearms touching the mat.

"One . . . two . . . three . . . four . . . ," she counts out.

By the time Kirby gets to "five" my stomach is cramping and I collapse onto the mat. Angel giggles until she starts snorting. Rather than punch her in her pretty face, I start laughing, too. I look so absurd, I just can't help it.

"Now we're going to a side plank," Kirby goes on. "This helps your obliques."

Kirby rolls onto her side and props herself up with her left elbow. "And hold it for ten."

Angel copycats her with ease while I struggle just to anchor my elbow, let alone defy gravity. "Lift up your hip from the floor, Emery!" Kirby yips. "Just like your sister."

"Now let's do the other side." She rolls over. And she counts down as I count the strands of muscle bulging from just under the skin of her stomach. I hate her.

"Next!" She claps three times. "Next, we are going to do some leg lifts. You are just going to put them up a few inches above the ground and hold them. This will really help your core." I cheat by bending my knees midair. I am remembering vividly why I hated cheerleading so much.

"Now we are going to do an extended crunch," she says. "Don't let your legs or arms touch the ground. You want to feel the tension in your core."

As we go through our workout, I can see Mom through a window in the lobby talking on the phone. She doesn't look happy. In fact, Mom has been acting very stressed out since last week when I pulled my stunt. Being a control freak, she doesn't like knowing whether or not I am making progress. She's forty-two and still hasn't figured out that life, by nature, is out of our control.

After our workout, my abs (or I assume they are my abs since I can't actually see them) are burning. Angel and I head to the cheerleader changing room.

As I'm slipping back into my clothes, Angel pulls a box from her gym bag and hands it to me.

"What's this?" I ask.

"The secret weapon," she replies.

I look at the box. "Herbal laxative tea. You want me to poop? That's disgusting."

"How do you think I stay so thin?"

"By not eating hardly anything and exercising like a total freak of nature."

"That's only part of it, little sis."

"What?" I read the ingredients, a bunch of Chinese herbs I can't pronounce. "You're drinking this stuff? Is it even legal?"

"Kendra gave me a box last year before my first bikini modeling shoot. I lost five pounds in a week, and ever since I have been addicted."

"Does Mom know?"

"I think so," she says. "But she never says anything. I think she thinks the end justifies the beans."

"The means," I correct her.

"Haha." Angel giggles. "Yeah, that's right. You know what I mean." She pulls one of the tea bags from the box. "Just drop it in some hot water and sip it. But be careful, it only takes a few hours for it to work its magic."

We both giggle. It almost reminds me of when we were little kids, when we did everything together. When we would wear the same little outfits to school. Before I got fat and she stayed skinny.

"Emery, I think you will need to do this to lose the fifty. But make sure you keep it on the DL. Doc won't allow it. They will say it is cheating. But, you know, it's really only cheating if you get caught."

"Okay, you're the expert." I take a sniff into the box. It smells like real tea that has been sitting in a rancid Dumpster for a few months. "How many of these a day should I drink?"

"Start with one at night." Angel scans the changing room, making sure no one is in earshot. "And if you think you can handle it, ramp up to another one just before lunch."

I stuff the box of tea into my backpack and slip on my sneakers. Before walking out, I look in the wall mirror. I turn and check out my 360.

"What's it like being skinny?" I ask Angel. "I mean, if I keep it up, I will need to know this."

"Honestly?" she says. "It's great sometimes. Like when you're at the beach, or wanting to look cute in clothes and stuff. It makes me feel more confident. But sometimes it can be a total curse."

"Yeah, I can only imagine that looking so hot in skimpy clothes and getting attention from all the guys has got to be so taxing on you. Sorry if I'm sounding bitter. But well, I am."

"I don't expect you to feel sorry for me," she says. "Like I said, it can be great. I do think my life is easier than yours in a lot of ways. And I'm not saying that to be mean. But as much as it might sound weird, it is also harder in some ways."

"Like how?"

"Like when I first got to Highland as a freshman. No one would talk to me. All the popular girls were threatened by me, probably because I wore cute little outfits and showed off my body. They were just jealous. But they hated me so much."

"They were just threatened by you," I say. "They're insecure bitches."

"I know, but I had to do everything I could to earn their trust. They were afraid I was going to steal their boyfriends. They just assumed that was my plan, and I had to prove I wouldn't."

I can't believe Angel and I are actually talking, confiding, having, like, a real heart-to-heart. I imagine this is what real, actual sisters do, not feuding bitches like we have been for so many years. And it feels nice.

Angel stands next me, checking herself out in the mirror. "It is so hard to stay skinny, Emery. So hard. Trust me, this is not my natural body type, what nature would have for me. The sad fact is that I have to skip meals all the time, watch everything I eat like an OCD psycho. I drink that tea." Angel looks as if she's about to cry. But she is able to maintain her pageant-queen stoicism. "It is so exhausting. Kendra and all those girls would turn on me the second I got fat. I wouldn't fit in. They wouldn't treat me the same. They wouldn't accept me. And of course, if I did get fat, I don't know how I would deal with Mom's—"

"Inspections," I finish her sentence.

"Exactly."

She pivots backward and cranes her neck to scope out her backside. "I've never told anyone this before, but when I look in a mirror like this, the first thing I see are the flaws, the stuff I don't like about my body. Like, right now, I see my ass and I hate it." She pokes her right butt cheek. "Look at the jiggle. It's all squish. It is so gross."

"Angel, that's insane. That is called a butt. It is supposed to have some fat. That's natural."

"I know that, but I hate it. I wish I didn't care so much, but I do. That's why I have always envied you. You just don't care."

"But I do care."

"Yeah, I know, but that's only now because you want to win the money. But you have always done your own thing."

"Well, breaking news: I am a sellout."

"Yeah, but you are selling out to save our family."

"What do you mean by 'save our family'?"

"I know about the foreclosure stuff," she says. "I saw the letter from the bank and confronted Mom. I respect you for what you're doing. You could have said no, but you said yes, and you're going through hell to keep us from being a bunch of hobos." She catches herself. "I mean, homeless individuals."

I smile. She continues, "And, Em. One last thing."

"Yeah?"

"Do you think Mom is cheating on Dad?"

"With Doc?"

Angel nods sullenly.

"I don't know, sis," I say. "And I kind of don't want to know."

As I'm about to open the door out to the lobby, I turn back to Angel.

"Oh, I wanted to tell you something. I've been meaning to tell you that I'm sorry for dropping that F-bomb on you."

"It's okay," Angel says. "Let's face it, I probably deserved it."

Angel and I leave the changing room and hop into a crew van for the ride back home. Instead of Ryan driving, there's a gruff guy with a gray beard and a potbelly behind the wheel.

"Excuse me, sir," I say, leaning forward from the backseat. "Where is Ryan?"

"Fired," the driver says.

"Fired? Why would Ryan be fired?"

The driver doesn't take his eyes off the road.

"Honey, I don't know. They just told me I'm the new PA."

"Not to be mean," I tell him. "But you're a little old to be called a 'new' anything."

"Then that's all well and good," he says. "Doc will be happy that you and I won't be flirting."

The moment we park in my driveway, I storm into the house, where we are scheduled to have a "brand meeting" with Doc, who is holding court on the back patio with a few agent-looking types in white shirts and ties.

"What happened to Ryan?" I rudely interrupt.

"Excuse me, dear, but we are in the middle of a meeting," Doc says.

"Why did you fire him?"

"This is not the time or place to get into this, Emery. On top of that, anything having to do with employee relations is confidential."

"Bullshit. You're a liar."

"Emery, you are being so out of line." Mom stands up. "You have to apologize right now. You have no idea what you're talking about."

Doc shoots a cold stare at Mom. "Please go deal with your daughter," he says.

Mom's eyes lock with Doc's. It's as if they are speaking to each other through their eye-cringing gazes. There is something going on between them, but I can't quite figure out what it is. An affair? Doc is far too doughy, crass, and unattractive for my mom. I simply can't imagine that. But I wonder. He is rich. But still. So gross.

They break their staring contest and suddenly Mom pulls me into the kitchen by the wrist and shakes me by the shoulders.

"Emery," she grunts. "Ryan was selling information to the paparazzi. That's why he was let go. He was telling them where you were going ahead of time. That's why there were so many photographers everywhere you went."

I feel the blood falling from my heart to my feet. The room starts spinning.

"Were there any paparazzi following you to and from cheer-leading today? No. You see? Doc is just trying to protect you. You're a celebrity now, Emery. People are going to try to take advantage of you. We need to tighten the circle of trust, and Ryan couldn't be trusted."

"So it had nothing to do with him flirting with me?" I ask.

"No, honey."

"Nothing at all?"

She gives me a hug. "Nothing at all."

Mom pulls back with a sympathetic glance. "When you're famous you become a target," she says. "Look at that *TV Weekly* story. That's just horrible how that was released."

"Oh, really?" I snap. "Horrible, huh? If you thought it was so horrible, why is this the first time you have even brought it up to me? I mean, wouldn't a real mom have comforted her daughter, have asked if I was okay? That was the worst day of my life."

"Honey, I knew you had Dr. Gen to work it out with. I wanted to respect your privacy."

I laugh maniacally. "Oh, that's a good one. Privacy?" I point to the camera mounted in the ceiling that is capturing this entire conversation. "If you cared about privacy we wouldn't be on this stupid reality show in the first place. You're a joke, Mom. A very unfunny joke."

I stomp over to the stove, fill a cup with water, and stick it in the microwave.

"Emery, that's not fair. We all agreed to this together, as a family. No one forced you to do anything. What does Dad say, 'Always the victim, never the victor.' That is not how you want to go through life!"

"Can't you see, Mom? Leave me alone. I am trying to have some privacy here. Some loser privacy."

Mom slinks back out to the patio, where I'm sure they're talking about how well the line of Freedom products are selling. How the Freedom Menu™ is all the rage. How the plans to open a chain of ClubFreedom™ health and fitness centers is right on schedule. How they have trademarked the phrase "New-and-Improved Emery." How Angel is getting hosting job offers from every TV show. How Dad's lecture-circuit agent's phone has been ringing off the hook.

But I don't care. All I care about is losing the fat that rattles like Jell-O around my legs, my hips, my stomach, my arms, my chin, and until it is no longer there, I will not be able to survive in this world that worships everything that is a thing. So all I care about is getting rid of it, cleansing myself of my past body, my past life. Maybe they're right. Maybe I will feel freedom finally. Maybe I will feel born again.

The microwave beeps. I grab the cup of steaming water and take it upstairs to my bedroom. I take a tea bag from the box in my backpack and drop it into the water, pressing the bag with a spoon. The clear water fades into a murky brown liquid that stinks like a rotten garden. I lift the cup to my lips, squeeze my nose with my thumb and forefinger, and sip the drink. And as my stomach begins to gurgle, I feel like I might be drinking the most putrid concoction ever created, but at least I am gaining some control over my body.

TUESDAY, DECEMBER 31 (DAY 30), 11:25 P.M. PST

I've never been a big fan of New Year's Eve. There's so much pressure that comes with it. First of all, you have to come up with a fancy party to attend. Which means you have to come up with something fancy to wear. Which means you are doomed to be in an uncomfortable outfit the entire night. And then comes the pressure of having to kiss someone at the stroke of midnight, which, seeing as though Ben and I have broken up and I am not exactly the hottest potato in the pot, is not going to happen. Not that anything is going to happen as I lie in bed by myself, sipping my poo-poo tea and watching Ryan Seacrest and thousands of others crammed into Times Square waiting for the crystal ball to drop and usher in a new year.

My phone buzzes. I pick it up.

Missing u, dork

It's Ben. I can ignore him like I have ever since I found out he was apparently being groomed to star in *To Catch a Predator*. But I suppose I could lift my boycott, if only temporarily, seeing as though it is New Year's Eve and all.

Hi Ben

ur alive!!! I saw ur vid blog. Of course, I forgive u. all that stuff in the magazine was before we met. I get it. don't worry. I would have done the same thing and not said anything.

2 nice to me. Im such a bitch sometimes.

We need 2 talk asap

No we dont ben. don't do this bennigan. I need space still.

but I have to tell u something important

then tell me now

cant on text

Why? Weirdo . . .

Just cant. Not safe

Did u join the CIA or something?

hahaha No but can we talk tmorw?

k

happy new year. Em.

u 2

WEDNESDAY, JANUARY 1 (DAY 31)

DD has graciously given me a day off from working out. Very, very charitable of my trainer. But he did suggest that I take a fast-paced walk, just to keep myself in what he calls "movement mode." DD keeps saying that "a body at rest tends to stay at rest and a body in motion tends to stay in motion." This, of course, is a basic law of physics, and apparently also a basic law of Big Girls. Not wanting to be a Big Girl, I have been being a Good Girl and listening to what he says.

I shuffle my size sevens downstairs in my tights and baggy tank top and find Dad sitting on the couch watching some college football game with the volume cranked up to an obnoxious level.

"Who's winning?" I ask.

"Oregon," he says with disgust. He doesn't take his eyes off the screen. "Seven to zip."

"Wanna go for a walk at the beach?"

"Um," he says, still not looking at me standing beside the couch. "Can we do it at halftime? USC is about to tie it up."

I shrug him off and walk to the kitchen to grab my "breakfast" before heading upstairs to shoot a new video blog. And by the time I come back downstairs, Dad has left the couch and the TV is off.

I go searching around the house and find Mom sunning herself by the pool. "Where's Dad?"

"Oh, he went for a run," she says. "He wanted to run now so he could be back in time to watch the second half."

"Did he mention anything about me?"

"Yes, sorry," she says, putting down her *Coastal Living*. "He said to tell you he wouldn't have time to walk. So sorry I forgot. I'm just enjoying not having the cameras around and turning my brain off for a while."

"Why aren't there cameras today?"

"Doc gave them a day off. It is a holiday, and he said we can just re-create anything that happens anyway."

"Gee, what a nice guy."

"He really is," she replies, my sarcasm soaring right over her head. "Doc means well."

Clearly having run out of semi-sane people to interact with, I break down and text Ben.

wanna hang out?

when? Where?

in 15. At our fave spot on pier

c u there. But PS: make sure no one follows you. This has to be on DL.

I go upstairs and take off my tights and slip into a pair of new workout stretch pants that make me look skinnier. In the mirror, I notice that they are loose around the butt and thighs. Before getting too excited, I remind myself that they're still a size Large. I put on a jogging bra and notice that it is also looser than normal. Glancing down over my boobs, I can see that, perhaps, I have lost one fat roll from my belly when I bend over.

I slide on a baseball cap and a pair of sunglasses, enjoying my stealth adventure. It has been twelve days since we broke up. While I don't plan on ever getting back together with Ben, it hasn't been easy going cold turkey either. He was my best friend, my confidant, the one-and-only other heavyweight at school who could understand what it is like to be an Other at Highland High. He was the yin to my yang. I trusted him. And then BOOM.

I suppose I also have some explaining to do to him. Okay, fine. A lot of explaining. When he and I began dating, I told Ben I was a virgin, which, since everything in the *TV Weekly* article was true, was a total lie on my part. At the very least, I owe him an apology.

I walk outside the front door and scan the street for paparazzi. You can tell the paps because their cars usually have tinted windows. And if they don't, you can always identify a pap car because some creeper will be sitting in the driver's seat fondling a camera. Luckily the street is clear on this holiday morning.

I walk down the sidewalk of side streets and turn right at the bike path that runs the length of the city beach north-south along the ocean. It is a quiet morning, and cold, too chilly to hang out at the beach. But there are still plenty of walkers, Rollerbladers, and random joggers around. I pull my hat down low, just to make sure no one recognizes me.

When I get to the concrete Highland Beach pier, I hang right and in the distance at the end, amid a few fishermen casting over the silver handrail, sits Ben on a bench. (He's not hard to spot. Being six-three and close to three hundred pounds makes you stand out a bit.)

The moment he spots me walking toward him, a wide smile spreads across his cute, chubby face. But I refuse to hug him. I've got too much pride to succumb to his adorableness after all that happened.

"Wow, you look good," he says.

I almost joke that I might be skinny enough for him to look at on the Web, but I really don't want to obsess over that any longer, even though I really am getting over it. I need to move forward, not let the past define me. Blah, blah, blah.

"Thank you," I say. "Starving will do that to you, I suppose."

"It's just nice to see you."

He goes to hug me, but I step back.

Ben looks away as a seagull flies on the railing and stands beak-first in front of us.

"Ever feel like someone is staring at you?" I crack.

"Or like someone is about to come poop on you," Ben jokes.

We share a laugh, which at least cuts the tension a little.

"I wonder what that bird is thinking?" Ben asks.

"I bet he's looking at us and wondering what it is we are eating to be so fat and is as jealous as hell. Only animals wish they were fatter."

"You don't have to make any jokes, Em."

"You're right, but I do have to apologize. I mean, I lied to you. I wasn't a virgin. I should have told you the truth."

"It's okay, Em. I forgive you. I totally understand. I really get it."

I sit on the bench beside Ben. We both sit looking past the sea gull out at the ocean waves breaking onto the shore. Ben's too nice to call me a lying slut. He did put the push in pushover, after all.

But while I normally would want him to man up, show some sack, and call me out, this time I'm glad he's just a plain and simple sympathetic human being.

"I saw a seal before you got here," Ben says. "They hover around the bait from these poles around here. Always looking for a free meal. The seals will only eat fish. They won't touch a plant. They're not like manatees."

"Neither are people," I say. "Manatees don't prey on others. Manatees don't hurt anything. They eat when they're hungry, sleep when they're tired, and swim when they want to just enjoy life."

"I miss those days we spent in Crystal River," Ben says. "In fact, I miss just being with you anywhere. That's why I have to tell you something very important. You need to know the truth. For your sake, for our sake. For your family's sake."

Ben drags his black backpack out from under the bench and pulls out his laptop. He rests it on his lap, but before flipping it open, asks, "You sure no one followed you here?"

"Yeah."

"Good."

Ben flips open the computer and opens up a video file.

"First of all," he begins, "you have to promise you will finally believe me after I show you this."

"Believe what?"

"That I was set up. That I haven't been surfing that nasty porn on my computer."

"Why should I believe that?"

"Because Ryan came to see me the other day," Ben says in a near whisper. He looks around again to make sure no one is eavesdropping. "He told me about everything. He told me the truth."

Ben pulls a tiny piece of plastic from his pocket. "And he gave me this thumb drive."

Ben starts looking around nervously. A few old guys are fishing off the rail about twenty feet down the pier. The seagull is the only being within earshot.

"Don't worry," I say. "Even Doc wouldn't be sleazy enough to put a hidden camera on a bird."

Ben straightens his leg and kicks it out, shooing away the winged stalker. "After you find out what I am about to tell you . . ." He scans the pier again like a paranoid freak. "You might want to reconsider that."

Ben sticks the thumb drive into the side port on his laptop and clicks on the video icon.

I want to make a joke that he's showing me his new porn collection, but given that Ben is sweating and has the most serious look I've ever seen on his adorable face, I opt for silence.

"Ryan was afraid to tell you because he knows you are being watched constantly, that there is always a camera or a microphone around. So he told me what is going on, hoping you'd find out. He signed an NDA, so he is very scared Doc could come after him."

"NDA."

"A Non-Disclosure Agreement. He is legally prohibited from sharing any secrets about the show, but he's so pissed about getting fired, he was willing to take the risk."

"So tell me what he said."

"Emery, Doc is the one who had Ryan surf those websites on my computer. They hacked into it right before you came by, distracting me with some crazy story about how I had to go outside and shoot an interview. While I was outside, Ryan says he surfed all those sites. It was a total setup." Ben shakes his head. "I mean, I don't even like skinny chicks."

"Honestly, Ben, you don't have to do this." I stand up and lean my elbows on the rail of the pier with my back to him. "I don't care if you are surfing those sites anymore. You're a teenage boy. This qualifies as a hobby for you idiots."

Ben springs up from the bench and grabs me by the shoulder. "Emery, I swear I'm telling you the truth. But to be totally honest, them hacking my laptop is the least important thing. So, please, just sit back down."

"Fine," I say, taking a seat under protest. "But I have to get back for my workout in fifteen minutes. So make it snappy, Benski."

"Here's the deal," Ben says, licking his upper lip. "Ryan gave me this video file. It's an interview with your mom that was conducted before *Fifty Pounds to Freedom* was started. It is some sort of casting tape that Ryan shot for Doc, but that Ryan was later ordered by Doc to delete. Well, by accident he never did. And now Ryan wants you to see this. And, Emery, so do I."

Ben places the computer in my lap and clicks **PLAY**.

I immediately recognize our living room couch Mom's sitting on as her casting interview begins.

"Tell me about Emery," a voice that is obviously Doc's says off camera.

"She's the youngest of my two daughters, and she is a real individual, let's just say that."

"In what way?" Doc asks.

"In every way. I've always admired that about her. She is a perfect mix of her mom and dad."

"How so?"

"For starters, she has a very clear take on life, much like I do. Now, of course, her take is totally different than mine might be on most things, but she is very passionate about her point of view. Like me."

"And exactly how is she like her father?"

Mom looks down with a nervous smile. "You could probably take a wild guess," she says, looking back up at, presumably, Doc. "She is very intelligent. Almost scary smart. She has a talent for being able to sum up a person the moment she meets them. She is, um, very intuitive like that."

"And who did you say she gets that from?" Doc asks.

"From her father," she tells him, looking down. She looks up and smiles. "She gets that from you."

I feel nothing. I am numb. I just sit staring at the video box as it continues playing but I no longer can even hear the words coming out of her mouth. Ben places his arm around me, but I only know this because I see it out of the corner of my right eye; I cannot feel him.

I gently close the laptop, pull out the thumb drive, and stand up and utter something like "Bye, Ben," but I don't even know what I say.

I start running—faster than I have ever run. Ben tries to catch up but within seconds he stops. He shouts at me, but I don't look back. I don't want to look back.

Doc is my father.

I sprint down the pier to the bike path and turn right, heading south, in the opposite direction of my house, the opposite direction of the pressure, the attention, the criticism, the secrets, the lies.

Doc is my father.

Ten minutes, twenty, thirty minutes go by, and I am still running. When I reach the end of the bike path, where it meets a steep cliff, I dart up the flight of stairs leading to the top of the cliff. And I keep running. Winding through a grove of eucalyptus trees, I sprint deep into the thickening stand of trees atop Point Verde, an isolated hill section above Highland Beach.

I haven't been to the very top of this path since I was a kid, when the man I thought was my father would take me up here on hikes, encouraging me to keep going because the view from the very top was well worth the effort. At least once a week in the summer, he and I would go on this hike. It was, in fact, the only time I can remember being alone with my dad as a kid, not having Angel or Mom distracting him from paying attention to me.

This memory is all that I can hold in my brain as I dodge the rocks in the dirt pathway, my lungs laboring for air, but nonetheless undeterred from continuing on. And some five minutes later, the steep incline begins to level out and leads to a flat outcropping of rock shaded by a lone, giant oak tree. Puffing and panting and gasping for air, I don't even bother to look at the stunning ocean view behind me. Rather, my eyes scan up and down the tree. And there it is—exactly what I've come to see.

At waist level, carved into the bark is the work of a nine-year-old girl with nothing but a Swiss Army knife and her innocence: *EMERY + DAD 4EVER*.

I trace my finger through the deeply carved letters before falling to my knees in exhaustion, staring into the distance until the first sun of the New Year goes down on the horizon.

IV.DESSERT

FRIDAY, JANUARY 3 (DAY 33)

The blue pills are round and tiny. But man, they sure pack a punch. Over two hours ago, just after breakfast, I took three of them and I have been doing sprint intervals on the beach with DD for over an hour straight. And I am not at all tired.

My trainer wants to know where I am getting all this new-found energy, especially since my daily calorie count has been well below a thousand despite all my increased exercise.

"Life," I lie, while the truth, however, is Adderall. "Life gives me energy." I bounce up and down like a pogo stick, noticing rather happily that not as much jiggles as it used to.

The pills sit in Mom's medicine cabinet, several bottles of them. So many, there is no way she would know I was sneaking a few a day from them. I couldn't sleep last night or the night before, or the night before that. In fact, every night, well, every day, all I can think about is how betrayed I feel. But I won't tell anyone I now know the truth. Instead, I will plot, plan, and secretly go ahead. I am in control.

Last night, around 3:00 a.m., I watched the rest of the interview with my mom.

"So why didn't you ever tell Emery the truth?" Doc asks.

"You know why, Docky."

"Of course, but tell it for the camera."

"Let me see," my mom says, taking a sip of water. "It is sort of, um, complicated. First of all, when you and I met on the set of *Baywatch*, it was a very tough time in my life. I was twenty-five years old and had a one-year-old baby, Angel. Looking back, I was a baby who had just had a baby. I wasn't ready for it, especially what it did to my body, and I wanted to get back to work modeling and acting. Jasper, as you know, by then had been traded to Utah, but I stayed back in Highland with Angel, all alone, trying to restart my career. Luckily I was young and my body bounced back pretty quickly, which is how I got cast by you for the *Baywatch* episode you were directing."

Mom looks sad as she tells the story. But she won't cry. I have never seen her cry. Ever. Her emotions are as bottled up as the prescriptions in her cabinet that I have raided.

"Then I got pregnant. Of course, it was all a mistake. We were caught up in the moment, the two of us. You and I knew that. We were on the same page when it came to keeping the affair a secret. So we never told Jasper. Or Emery for that matter."

"Does your husband have any inkling that Emery is not his daughter?"

"Yes, I think he does," Mom answers. "But I can't say for sure."

"Why do you think he does?"

"Because Emery is so different than him. You know, physically. And she's not petite like me or Angel. But we don't ever talk about it. In fact, we don't talk about a lot of things anymore."

"That's sad, I'd imagine."

"Um, yeah, but that's why I think doing this show could be a good thing for our family. It will bring us together again. And it will bring out the truth."

"How so?"

"Well, I think your idea is a good one," she says. "We will tell Emery and Jasper after the finale. I know it might sound crazy, but I feel like it will be easier to break the news to Emery and Jasper in front of millions of people. I don't know why exactly. Maybe just because I know they won't freak out as much."

"How do you expect Jasper will take it?" Doc asks.

"He will be angry, but in my heart of hearts, I hope he will forgive me. This is a sixteen-year-old mistake I made."

A mistake. I am a mistake!

"And what about Emery? How will she react?"

"Emery is strong."

I'm thinking of her interview as I do more beach sprints, hoping to push the thoughts out of my mind. Meanwhile my heart feels as if it will pound through my chest and I am sweating gallons. I am dizzy. But I keep on sprinting, from one lifeguard tower to the next, with a one-minute break in between, sipping water (zero calories). We are on our nineteenth repetition. The last two days, we did twenty-five reps. My energy is through the roof. This. Girl. Is. On. Fire!

"You are lookin' good!" DD enthuses. "Just look at those thighs. So tight!"

Normally I could slap my saddlebags and count "one Mississippi, two Mississippi" and watch them jiggle like Jell-O. DD slaps my bare thigh, and it causes barely a ripple.

"How much do you think I weigh?" I ask DD. He looks me up and down and walks a full 360 around me as I stand in the sand. "I'd say one hundred sixty-five," he guesses. "Give or take a few pounds."

I quickly do the math. The goal is to get down to 149 pounds, so that means I have sixteen days to lose sixteen more pounds—that is, if DD's estimate is accurate. It also would mean I am right on schedule: a pound a day. I can do this.

"Are you sure?" I ask him.

"Honey," DD replies. He lifts up his shirt and tightens his six pack. "This is what I do for a living. Fitness is my business."

The tabloids certainly don't have a consensus. Every major celebrity magazine, in a display of a total lack of creativity or distinction, had some sort of "expert" analyzing photos of me.

> *Star* = 173 pounds
>
> *Us* = 175 pounds
>
> *People* = 166 pounds
>
> *National Enquirer* = 154 pounds (along with the headline: SHE'S ROTTING AWAY!)[12]

Obviously I would like to know how much I weigh. But if I am caught weighing myself, not only will I not win the million bucks, but per my agreement, I will have to pay THE

---

[12] I wish.

NETWORK a million dollars for breach of contract. So I'm just left wondering. And starving.

By the time midnight rolls around, I am still a bundle of energy. And because I don't sleep anymore, I walk at night when everyone else is sleeping. It's the only time the cameras aren't around, the only time I have by myself. I can walk down the bike path at the beach in peace, mostly thinking about what I am going to do when this is all over. But this life, my coming "after-life," is my secret. I also have a lot of conversations in my head. With Dad. With Doc. With Mom. I sometimes talk them out like a crazy person. Luckily no one is around. Just me. It helps. But I'm still hurting. A lot.

These midnight walks also allow me to have shady meet-ups with Ben. He refuses to go back on camera, so even though we are "back on," I am letting the world think we aren't. I would die without him. I would still be living without the knowledge that I am the product of a cheap Hollywood affair, not a sweet romance. And my body is the product of a man's genes that, for better or worse, explain a lot about my physique.

I resemble my biological father in many obvious ways:

- Pear shape

- Pale skin

- Dark, deep-set eyes

- Thick legs

- A roll of fat around my waist

Luckily, I got zero of his personality and that pretentious British accent. But so much has been out of my control, and I didn't even know it.

Thank God for Ryan. Thank God for Ben. Knowledge is power, indeed.

I get to the pier and in the distance I see Ben, sitting on his usual bench. It's a clear night, a near full moon casting long shadows onto the concrete pilings.

"There she is," he says when he sees me approaching. "The incredible shrinking girl."

"In the flesh!" I say. "The loose flesh."

"Seriously, Em." Ben gives me a bear hug so gentle I melt into his chest. "I barely recognize you anymore."

"Good. That's the idea here."

"Just be careful," he cautions. "I don't know how you're doing it, but the pounds are just melting off you. It's just not worth it."

That's what speed, laxative tea, starvation, and obsessive exercise tend to result in. I can't tell him this. This is my secret that I control. This is my body. They can take away my soul one big lie at a time, but they can't take away my body. I control my body.

"So when are you going to confront your mom and Doc?"

"Not now. Definitely not now."

"You have to sometime."

"Not until this show is over. I don't want to give him the satisfaction of making so-called 'good TV.'"

"Have you heard from Ryan at all?"

"Yeah," Ben says. "He wanted me to tell you that he's sorry he had to break the news to you. And he says Doc has planned a big reveal for some Emery Tells All special the night after your weigh-in."

"Great. Can't wait."

We both giggle. No one but the two of us has a clue what's about to go down.

WEDNESDAY, JANUARY 8 (DAY 38)

THE NETWORK has set up a full day of interviews at my house with the media to promote the live finale of *Fifty Pounds to Freedom* on January 19. Rather than doing the final weigh-in from my little living room, they have rented out the Staples Center in downtown L.A. and are charging fifty dollars a ticket to fans who can prove they have signed up for ClubFreedom™. Raymond has informed me that the finale is already sold out, that there will be over eighteen thousand people there, and like fifty million watching at home. "It will be like the Super Bowl of fat," I respond.

Raymond shrugs his shoulders and says, "I guess."

To promote this extravaganza, THE NETWORK has invited fifteen journalists from the biggest media outlets—five magazines, five TV shows, and five websites—to come interview me and Doc together. Each interviewer gets ten minutes to ask us anything they want.

What has been the best and worst thing about being on the

show? (Getting skinny is best and having to do nothing but try to get skinny is the worst) . . . What do you plan to do with the money? (Half to my family, half to myself) . . . Why do you think viewers are so captivated by your journey? (Because I am being honest and real and people appreciate that) . . . Will you and Ben ever get back together? (I don't know) . . . Has the show brought you closer as a family? (In some ways, yes, and in other ways, no).

The questions lobbed our way aren't exactly the stuff of hard-hitting investigative reporting. Doc and I have been sitting here, side by side, since eight o'clock this morning and by noon I'm ready for a break.

As I sit in the kitchen eating a couple slices of turkey and a sliced tomato, Raymond sits down next to me. "You're doing an awesome job, just perfect," he says. "You are giving them answers, but not really anything of substance. It is the perfect celebrity interview. We, of course, want to keep saving your best stuff for the show. We can't give away the Best of Emery for free!"

I roll my eyes and take a swig of water. "I aim to please."

"Good stuff," Raymond says. "The next interview, in about fifteen minutes, is with Jake McHenry from *Access Showbiz*. He's a big fan of yours. He's been covering you with daily reports."

When I sit back down, I recognize him instantly from television. At least pushing forty, Jake wears nerd-style plastic frame glasses, and short hair that spikes up on top. I've been watching him on TV shows giving his commentary since I was a little kid. I remember seeing that he was friends with the

Kardashians, so I take it that covering reality whores is his specialty.

"A pleasure to finally meet you," Jake says, shaking my hand. He reaches to shake Doc's hand and Doc reciprocates with his usual limp grab-and-shake.

"Shall we get started?" Doc, always the producer, suggests.

Jake gets right into it.

"Doc, there is no question that *Fifty Pounds to Freedom* has been a runaway ratings hit," he begins.

"Why, yes, it certainly has."

"But it also is coming under a lot of criticism."

"It is?"

"Yes, as a matter of fact," Jake says, thumbing through a stack of stories.

"And what are these supposed critics saying?" Doc asks with a weak smile.

"A common criticism is that the show sets an unhealthy example for teenage girls—all women as a matter of fact— who are struggling with their weight. The very title suggests you have to be thin to be happy. Is that the message you are sending?"

Doc sits up straight. "I'd counter that we are setting a positive example, that Emery here is a brave role model for the invisible masses. She is an inspiration."

Jake locks eyes with me and I grin slightly.

"Emery is brave, I agree," Jake says. "She has been quite inspiring in her dedication. But for example, a leading expert from the Council of Diet and Exercise says that Emery's restricted, low-calorie diet and extreme exercise regimen, coupled with a very rapid weight loss, is a very dangerous example to be setting. How do you respond to these critics?"

Raymond steps in between the camera and Doc, waving his hands. "Okay, let's stop here. We need to keep the questions to the show. You knew the rules, Mr. McHenry."

"But I am asking very relevant questions about the show," Jake says.

Doc sits passively as Raymond instructs the audio engineer to unclip the mic from Jake's shirt.

"Wait," Jake says. "Just one quick question for Emery."

"No, sir, you have worn out your welcome. This is a publicity junket, not *60 Minutes*."

"Emery," Jake says, ignoring my jittery publicist. "Do you think the show is exploiting you in any way? Has the California labor department contacted you about any violations? About how many hours they are making you work?"

Doc leaps up from his chair and grabs Jake by the shirt, lifting him to his feet. "How dare you come into Emery's house at our invitation and ask such insulting questions?" Doc pushes Jake past the camera to the doorway. "You call yourself a journalist? You're a hack."

Jake bats away Doc's arms and steps back. "I'm just trying to find out the truth. I'm simply asking questions, looking for the truth."

Doc wipes a pond of sweat off his forehead and rubs it onto his pant legs.

"After all," Jake adds, "the truth shall set you free."

THURSDAY, JANUARY 9 (DAY 39)

Finally, a workout I actually want to do.

I'm getting a freerunning lesson with Jessica LaClair, the lady I saw on the late-night infomercial two months ago. She was leaping around an obstacle course using nothing but her body—climbing over walls, flipping over a car, jumping from one rooftop to another—and I felt inspired. Now that I have dropped some serious L-Bs, and thus feel like I can actually jump higher than an ox, I signed up for a lesson at Jessica's training gym in the Valley and, naturally, the camera crew is with me to document my attempt at testing out my new body.

"First of all," Jessica tells me as we stand on the mat in the middle of the gym. She stares up and down at my tights. "You need to dress like a freerunner. Let's get you something a little bit more comfortable. In this gym, we don't care about how you look, but that you have freedom of motion."

I'm already liking this place.

Jessica extends her sculpted right arm forward and hands

me a pair of gray cotton sweatpants right out of a 1950s phys ed class that I change into in the bathroom. By the time I come out, she has placed a three-foot-high foam block in the middle of the mat.

"The art of Parkour and freerunning is all about getting from point A to point B in the fastest, most efficient way possible," she says.

"So then we are going to drive in a car?"

"Very funny," she replies. "But, actually, a car is not very efficient. Most cars use gasoline, which is one of the most inefficient fuels in the world, and that gas is converted into energy using an internal combustion engine, which is also very inefficient. There is nothing more efficient than the human body."

Jessica stands about five feet in front of the foam block.

"Emery, in life what do you do when you encounter an obstacle?"

"Well, I used to just avoid them."

"And how did that work out for you?"

"I got fat and bitter."

"Right. But when you face your obstacles and get over them, you feel better about yourself. It's no different here. This block is in my way, and the best method to get over it is to execute a move called a speed vault. Watch."

Jessica runs at the block, presses her left palm flat onto it, giving her enough support to lift up her legs and whip them forward over the block in one fluid motion.

"Like a hurdler," she says. "But with some help from your hand. Give it a try."

The block goes up to my waist. It is high enough to require

some athleticism. But low enough that it is do-able. I can do this.

I run toward it and, doing my best to copy Jessica's form, press down with my left hand and spring my legs upward and over the block—albeit much less gracefully than Jessica. Yet I am so pumped that I fist pump into the air like I've just won *American Ninja Warrior*.

SATURDAY, JANUARY 11 (DAY 41)

The surgeon grins creepily and welcomes me in the lobby of his Beverly Hills office. But Doc doesn't like how he shook my hand.

"Too formal," he explains.

We do a retake.

"Emery, so nice to meet you!" the short, little doc in a white coat repeats.

"For the second time," I grumble.

"Cut!" Doc stomps around the cameraman. "Emery, this is the first meeting, so let's act like it is, please. Do it again."

After a successful Fake Take three, Dr. Creeper escorts me down the hall and into a room where I sit down on an examination table. He asks me to strip down naked to my panties and put on a gown. Luckily the heat is turned up. All those housewives who come here for their weekly touch-ups must have complained about the temperature at some point.

The surgeon has me stand naked in front of the table as he marks up my body with circles and X's on my hips, arms, thighs, stomach, neck, back, and butt. Our cameraman quietly sits in the corner shooting his scribble session.

"We can tighten all this up, no problem," the doctor says, shaking my muffin-top region. He grips onto it with both hands like it's a tube of salami. "There is a lot of loose skin in all the usual places, and as you keep losing more weight, this problem will only get worse. But tightening it up, a little body contouring, will make you bikini ready. You will be more confident."

He takes some pictures of my body parts, noting where he has placed his marks.

"See, Emery . . ." He grabs a fistful of my thigh flesh and lifts it toward my belly. "I can pull all this up, sew it into here in the groin, and then cut out all the remaining fat. Your legs will be half the size. Gorgeous."

"Will I have legs like Carrie Underwood?" I ask, facetiously. But he thinks I am serious.

"When I am done, you will have legs like Miley Cyrus, J Lo, Rihanna, and Carrie combined!"

I am speechless. For once.

"Okay, now," he continues. "Let's take a look up top."

I tuck my chin and gaze down as he starts cupping my breasts, squeezing them like he's testing tomatoes at the supermarket.

"I know, I know. They're very sag-a-licious."

"Nothing some implants can't remedy!" he says brightly. "They're really not so bad. Clearly your nipples are pointing downward and starting to droop and your breasts are stretched out from your prior weight gain, thus the stretch marks. You're lucky you weren't very big to begin with. This is a very manageable situation, don't you worry one bit."

He gets up from his chair and stands in front of me. "But, Emery, now *this* is a whole other issue we need to talk about." He looks closely at my face and starts pulling at the skin on my forehead. "Have you ever considered Botox?"

"What?"

"Botox. You know what that is, don't you?"

"Of course, but where would I need Botox?"

"Here." He presses into my temple near my eyes, scrawling a few points on each side. Then he does the same to the faint wrinkles on my forehead. "And here." He moves his fingers down to my smile lines and presses the marker into there, too. "You grew up at the beach, out in the sun a lot. This is very common. I see it all the time. It's not a 911-emergency type of situation, but it wouldn't hurt to get ahead of the inevitable. You know, premature aging . . ."

"You're joking, right?" I say.

"It's never too early for what I like to call proactive prevention. All the young celebrities, anyone who is famous and under twenty-five basically, is doing it."

My face has always been the one thing I didn't hate. I might have been fat, but at least I had a pretty face. Now this quack wants to nip and tuck me like a Highland Beach housewife?

Unable to muster a response, I just stare into his eyes. Dr. Creeper wears black-and-gold-framed glasses, and in his lenses I catch my reflection. That's when it hits me. And by "it" I mean everything: The totality of the tragedy that my life has become. I don't like the girl I see. She isn't the girl who has been making videos telling other girls to just learn to love themselves. She isn't the girl who always prided herself on being different, not succumbing to the peer pressure to fit in like everyone else. She isn't Emery. No.

She is a monster and this creep in a white lab coat is Dr. Frankenstein.

I shake my gaze off his glasses and quickly start getting my clothes back on over my marked-up body.

"We're not quite yet done with your exam, Ms. Jackson," he says. "Please let me finish up a few things so we can schedule a surgery date."

By now, I have buttoned my jeans and slipped on my sandals.

"Sir, I looked up the definition of freedom the other day. It said freedom is the power or right to act, speak, or think without restraint. But you wanna know something? It said nothing about saggy boobs or loose thighs."

When I walk past the surgeon, I realize I have forgotten something. "Oh, one other thing," I snap. "You've got a pretty big spare tire down there." I step toward him and grab hold of his middle-aged jelly belly. "But, you know, don't bother with getting lipo. My advice is that you just learn to love it."

I ignore Doc with a Heisman hand up to his face as he follows me out of the office and down the hallway. "Emery, we're doing the surgery. It is in the contract."

I press the elevator button. "Doc, how do you look yourself in the mirror at night and not be totally disgusted with yourself? I mean, seriously, how can you live knowing you're such a horrible human being?"

He shakes his head. "That's not true, my dear!"

I want to tell him I know the truth. That I know all about the Big Lie that he and Mom share and they are planning to ambush me, Dad, and Angel with it just over a week from now. I know because Ryan has told this to Ben, revealing that Doc said he is only doing this reality show so that my Mom won't sue him for child-support payments.

Yeah, this show is about freedom—his freedom from having to take responsibility for banging a married woman and getting her pregnant!

I want to tell him to his puffy face that I know that, as revolting as the thought is, he is my dad. I want to tell him that what's about to go down at next Sunday's finale is the result of me having an epiphany.

But I don't say anything more. Instead, I step inside the elevator and don't look back. I walk quickly out to the street, and when I see there are no cabs to hop into I run east down Wilshire Boulevard, as fast as I can, leaving the camera crew in the dust. I dart into the lobby of the Four Seasons hotel, and realizing I left my phone at Creeper Surgeon's office, borrow the phone from the front desk clerk and call Ben.

"Ben, let's do this," I say.

"Now?"

"It is time to start making it happen. You've called them, right?"

"Yes," he says. "We spoke. They are excited."

It will take Ben at least forty-five minutes to get from Highland Beach to the hotel. That leaves me plenty of time.

I walk over to the hotel restaurant and get seated in a private booth near the back so no one recognizes The Emery Jackson.

There is one thing about this New Emery that I don't resent. This girl doesn't run off to some fast-food palace and stuff her face with food that only makes her feel worse about herself. Instead, this Emery has a healthier plan.

I sit and order from the polite waiter a half-pound hamburger (medium rare) on a sesame seed bun. Lettuce, tomato, onions on the side. No cheese. No mayo. And since it has been over a month since I last enjoyed a hamburger, I am going to savor every bit of the ritual. I add in a small basket of fries, but also a side salad as a starter. Rather than a glass of soda, I order water with lemon.

This is my choice.

When the food arrives, I eat deliberately, chewing every piece entirely before swallowing. I eat the salad, and I am not even halfway through the cheeseburger and a few fries in when I have to stop because my shrunken stomach feels totally full. A minute later, I wash down my last bite with water and let out a deep breath. Dessert follows as a delicious bowl of mixed berries.

I don't feel shame. I don't feel stuffed to the point of stomach pain and embarrassing gaseous releases. For the first time I can remember I had myself a balanced, healthy four-course meal.

MONDAY, JANUARY 20 (DAY 50), 5:59 P.M. PST

According to the promos that have been running nonstop on THE NETWORK, the *Fifty Pounds to Freedom* finale promises to be "the most dramatic series finale in TV history."

One girl . . . Fifty pounds . . . Will she finally win her freedom from fat? Tune in Sunday at 9:00 p.m. to find out!

The show is a minute away from delivering on its promise of drama, but it's not gonna be of the kind everyone is expecting.

Thousands of fans have lined up outside the Staples Center, ringing around the arena on the sidewalk carrying signs and chanting my name—their own self-esteem somehow connected to my attempt at achieving something that fifty days ago seemed almost impossible. But over these last fifty days I have learned that my ability to pack on the pounds was the result of not only nurture[13], but also nature[14]. I learned that I was never going to have the skinny-bitch genetics of my mom or Angel. Or

---

[13] Taco Bell, etc.
[14] Doc = My dad.

the natural athleticism of my dad. But even before I was aware that my own body type and metabolism came from the sloppy DNA of Marvin "Doc" Harris and not the svelte Jasper Jackson, I embarked on this weight-loss journey.

Along the way, I learned a lot of good habits—mostly how to exercise and how to eat a healthy diet. Unfortunately, I have also developed what could best be described as an eating disorder. Taking laxatives and popping speed and obsessively reducing my calories to insanely low levels was, in retrospect, the most unhealthy thing I could have ever done. And it wasn't until I sat in that examination room being prodded and fondled by Dr. Frankenstein that I realized just how much I had lost myself in this stupid game. That's why, for this finale, things are about to get dramatic indeed.

Not because I'm about to step on a scale and find out if I have reached my goal of 149 pounds, which would mean I lost fifty pounds in fifty days and will instantly be showered with a million dollars.

But because no one in the arena knows what's about to happen.

Not Doc, who stands anxiously in his tux on the stage running through his lines in the prompter.

Not Lana Sinclair and her network cronies who are huddled with sponsors in a suite just left of the stage, no doubt counting the cabbage they've made off my struggle as they sip wine and toast their ratings success.

Not Angel, who cuddles next to Dad in the front row, biting her fingernails just like Mom has taught us.

And not Mom, who must be frantic backstage.

The lights go down in the arena and a video starts rolling on the big screen draped down the back of the stage. It's one of those slickly produced, cheesy montage videos that shows all the highs and lows throughout the last fifty days. There's me face-planting into the sand during my first beach run . . . my first weigh-in . . . crying in therapy with Dr. Gen . . . flirting with Ryan . . . signing autographs for a gaggle of crazed fans . . . undergoing my plastic surgery preop exam . . . the night Ben and I broke up and I totally lost my marbles.

Twenty million people are watching on TV. Twenty thousand watch inside Staples.

But not me and Ben. Instead, I'm slouched in seat 22A on Delta flight 2134, disguised in a trucker hat and giant sunglasses. When the doors are shut, I close the *50 Pounds Live* app I've been watching, turn off my phone, and stuff it into the seat pocket in front of me.

But then I realize I have one last thing to do. I pull my phone out and turn it back on, hoping it boots up before the flight attendants announce the cabin doors are closed.

Luckily, it only takes thirty seconds to get bars, and I quickly tap out and send what I plan to be my last tweet as a skinny, famous and—now, thankfully—madly in love girl: *the difference between being ugly and beautiful has zero to do with your appearance.*

A few minutes later, the jet speeds down the runway and we take off. As I look out my window at the L.A. city lights below, soaring above the clouds, now headed due East, I squeeze Ben's hand and smile as I realize this is just the beginning of my next great adventure.

Finally, I feel free.

TWO MONTHS LATER . . .

SURPRISE! I AIN'T DEAD . . . YET

I had told myself I would simply escape, that I would fly off into the sunset, disappear for a while to the only place I felt like I could be myself. But I guess I underestimated how hard it would be for me to leave you—my family, my fans, my loyal vlog followers—with so many unanswered questions. It wasn't very mature of me. Honestly, it was entirely irresponsible and gutless on my part. That's why I'm making this video.

In the interest of full disclosure, I have to warn you right off the bat that I won't have answers to all your questions, including but not limited to: Why so many little girls go through a "Princess Phase" . . . Why high schools make you take math class when computers can do it all anyway . . . Why no one has yet invented tasty food that doesn't make you fat . . . Why Taylor Swift is more famous than Hillary

Clinton . . . And why, even in this post-Apple era, it is still so hard to pour ketchup from a bottle. But don't be discouraged, kids. Eventually I will answer the greatest question plaguing young people today: how someone can get skinny, famous, and fall madly in love.

But first, let me explain where I've been. Because some of you might have believed the rumor that I've been holed up in a cabin outside of Buffalo, New York. Or that I've been held hostage in a bunker in Afghanistan. Everyone, it seems, has had theories, including the big kahuna theory that I'm deader than Elvis. Obviously, this one isn't true because—hello!—here I am.

I've been writing a book. Well, it's more of a diary. I needed to write it because there was simply too much to for me to explain in just a video.

It's quite peaceful here, as close to living off the grid as you can get these days. No paparazzi. No reality-show cameras. No one making me feel as if the only path to freedom is to change my appearance and look the like the girls on the cover of magazines. No biological dads, no checked-out nonbiological dads, no crazy moms. No drama.

Despite breaching my contract by going MIA right before the finale, I'm pretty sure that the ugly truth about *Fifty Pounds to Freedom* revealed in my book will free me from ever having to do another reality show again, especially with Doc. The government, I'm told, is already investigating him for making me, a minor, work all those hours (thanks to

Mr. McHenry's exposé). And when people read about just how shady and staged our show was, I'm sure this will be his last "reality" show, anyway.

Will I try to have an actual father-daughter relationship with Doc? Hold on while I force my breakfast back down my throat. Okay, vomit averted. The answer is not now. I'm too angry. Too hurt. I will give it time and, well, just take it from there. I wish I could tell you I was so evolved that I could forgive and forget. Much like losing weight when you love food and hate exercise, coming to grips with Doc being my dad has been quite the daunting task.

I truly wish I could tell you there is a perfect little ending to my story. I wish I could tie it all up in a bow like in the movies and tell you that I have had a Big Cry with Mom and Dad, and that we will get through this as a family, that time has begun healing the wounds that have been inflicted over the last sixteen years. But I can't. Not yet, at least. I will leave the Hollywood endings to Hollywood.

I made a lot of rookie mistakes, but I also did a lot of things right. Life is like that. Nothing is ever perfect.

But maybe now at least I can start from scratch. With expectations that are realistic. And healthy. This means no more diets, no more obsessive exercising, no more pills, no more weigh-ins, no more letting other people make me feel bad about myself. No more trying to act and look like someone I am not and can never be. No more compromising myself in order to make money. And, most important, no more secrets.

Soon I'll have to head back to Highland Beach and put together the pieces of the broken puzzle that is my life. I have been helping out on a tour boat that goes through the hot springs where manatees migrate during the winter, hiding here as a refuge from the cold harshness of the world. Just. Like. Me.

These sea cows have reminded me how to live a happy life: Eat when I'm hungry. Sleep when I'm tired. And in between, just enjoy the freedom of being alive.

addressed in this story. They are my heroes to whom this story is a tribute.

Plus there are so many special people in my life, the Author Enablers, who help me stay focused, informed, healthy, grounded, and inspired. This includes all the loyal fans and followers on social media who support everything I do. Quite simply, to name everyone on Team Ken would turn this section into something resembling a phone book. On top of that, I fear I would forget someone and, well, feel really stupid.

So, to cover all my bases, I would simply like to extend a sincere expression of gratitude to each and every one of you. Namaste.

Acknowledgments

How could I possibly thank the multitudes of friends, family members, colleagues, confidantes, and just plain old kind-hearted people who helped make this novel happen?

There are the obvious this-book-wouldn't-exist-without-you mentions, principally my agent, Michael Bourret, and my editor, Lisa Cheng. And, of course, my family—Brooke, Jackson, Chloe, and Bailey—who tolerate, encourage, and love me.

But honestly, from here the list grows so long it is somewhat paralyzing.

There are the friends who opened up to me about their struggles with weight, body image, and their personal food fight. The neighbor who selflessly did the same and to whom I am eternally grateful. The Crystal River manatees. The health professionals who offered their insights and brilliance just because they wanted me to get it right. The countless real-life weight-loss warriors who endure daily battles with many of the issues